Warwickshire County Council

NEW STK 7/21			
			J
men 6/3/24			

This item is to be returned or renewed before the latest date above. It may be borrowed for a further period if not in demand. **To renew your books:**

- **Phone the 24/7 Renewal Line 01926 499273 or**
- **Visit www.warwickshire.gov.uk/libraries**

Discover ● Imagine● Learn ● *with libraries*

Warwickshire County Council

Emma Rea lives in London and spends as much time as she can in Wales. After graduating from St Andrews with a degree in Russian, she worked as a magazine editor, as a trader in newsprint, and in publishing.

She brought her children up in Powys, inspired by childhood memories of Pembrokeshire and her grandmother's stories of growing up in Mumbles.

Emma is the author of middle-grade novel, *Top Dog* (Gomer) which was shortlisted for the North Somerset Teachers' Book Award.

EMMA REA

MY NAME IS RIVER

Firefly

First published in 2020
by Firefly Press
25 Gabalfa Road, Llandaff North, Cardiff, CF14 2JJ
www.fireflypress.co.uk

A CIP catalogue record of this book is available from
the British Library.

3 5 7 9 8 6 4 2

ISBN 9781913102142

*This book has been published with the support of
the Welsh Books Council.*

For Dougal

ONE

'A treehouse. Big enough to sleep in,' Dylan said, stabbing a fishfinger. He dropped a bit of it down to Megs when no one was looking.

'You'll need planks,' his dad said.

Dylan had thought of that.

'Can we have those ones in your workshop, leaning up against the back wall?'

'Guess you'll be wanting to use all my tools as well,' Dad said with a sigh, but he was smiling.

'Can I sleep in it?' Tommo asked, burying a pea in his mashed potato. Tommo always said you could swallow almost anything if it was buried in mash.

'Won't you be scared?' Dylan's mum asked, keeping a close eye on the peas. 'I wouldn't want you to change your mind and start wandering about at midnight.'

1

Tommo nodded. 'Yes, but if Dyl and the others are there, I'll be OK.'

'It could be ready by half-term. We can...'

Dylan's dad's phone rang.

Everyone looked at each other.

'Is it him?' Mum asked.

'It is,' Dad said, standing up so suddenly his chair fell over backwards. He pressed answer. 'Hello?' He reached out and placed a hand on Dylan's mum's shoulder.

Dylan felt a grin spread over his face. Mum was gazing at Dad, one hand over her mouth. Tommo's eyebrows had shot up and his mouth was open. Dad's eyes shone like they did after he'd helped a ewe through a difficult birth and a perfect lamb emerged, and struggled to its feet. Dylan stared at his dad, waiting. It couldn't take Owen long to say it.

Except something seemed to be wrong.

His dad was frowning.

'What do you mean?' his dad said, leaving the kitchen.

'Eat up, boys,' Mum said, still smiling. 'There's probably more paperwork to be done. These things take ages.'

So Dylan and Tommo finished up while Dad strode around the garden, phone clamped to his ear.

The strange thing was, Dad looked confused. Then angry. He started waving his arms around. Seeing that he was being watched from the kitchen window, he moved away to the back of the house.

Dylan exchanged a glance with his mum and he knew

they both thought it might be more than just extra paperwork. The phone call went on while Tommo had his bath. It was still going on when Tommo lined his cars up by his pillow. And now Dylan was eyeing his dad from the bathroom window, mouth full of toothpaste, with a heavy feeling in his stomach. A call that took this long couldn't be good.

He spat the toothpaste out and rinsed his toothbrush. He replaced it slowly in the rack, keeping his eyes on his dad, striding around the back garden in the dusk.

He was just wiping his mouth with his towel when his dad dropped his phone on the grass.

In slow motion, his dad raised both hands and locked them together on the back of his head. He leant back, as if to call out to someone in the sky. Then his chest expanded and even through the bathroom window Dylan could hear his roar. It went on and on, until it petered out into what you could only call a howl.

Dylan swallowed. His whole body went cold.

And then, like a folding chair, his dad collapsed down onto his haunches. He stayed like that, hands over his head, rocking. It was as if his whole body was flooded with oil and he'd stalled, just like an engine.

Dylan didn't know what to do.

He couldn't just go to bed.

He stood very still, and listened. When he was sure his dad was back inside, he crept out of the bathroom to hide behind the kitchen door.

'What on earth's happened, love?' his mum was asking.

When his dad spoke, his voice was dead. All the anger had gone. He might have been telling Mum he'd just put the bins out.

'The farm's been sold to someone else.'

'What? That's impossible. Bill said…' Mum sounded as confused as Dylan felt. What was Dad talking about? Today was the day Dad was to buy the farm his family had worked on for generations.

'Yeah. Bill promised to sell it to us. But now he's gone, it's up to the executors. Turns out he was in debt. They needed a better price.' He sighed a sigh that came all the way from his boots. 'Some cruddy global healthcare company made them an offer they couldn't refuse.'

'What do they –'

'Moss. They want to grow moss. What does it matter? It's all over, love.'

'Moss? But why our farm? Why ours?' His mother's voice broke and collapsed into a strangled cry.

'Apparently BlueBird buys up parcels of land all over the world to develop new products. It's ridiculous. There's any number of farms in Wales for sale – Evans has been trying to sell his for a year. Owen's written emails and made phonecalls all day long but thousands of people work for BlueBird and it's not easy to get through to the see-ee-oh. Anyway, it's done.'

'But we have rights. They can't just…'

'That's the worst of it, love. Apparently I signed away

the rights when we took on that extra field.' He gave a bitter laugh.

'This house, the garden, the fields, your polytunnels, the river, it all belongs to BlueBird now. We will never own it, and we can't even rent it any more. They don't want tenant farmers on it.'

Dylan didn't understand. Why wasn't Dad saying anything about how to get it back?

'All those years...' his mum's voice trembled. 'All our saving. Your efforts, your grandfather's, your father's...'

There was a long silence. Dylan strained to listen, but his parents seemed to have turned to stone.

'I can't face telling the boys yet,' Dad said, eventually. 'Tommo's too young to understand, but Dylan...'

'Dylan will...' His mum, his cheerful, sensible, no-nonsense mum actually began to cry.

'I know. He loves every blade of grass on this farm. Let's just say there's been a delay until we know what we're doing.' His dad groaned a long, horrible groan. 'We've got until Christmas.'

Dylan tiptoed away, his brain boiling over.

Very quietly, he let himself out through the front door and padded off barefoot, with Megs at his heels, towards the riverbank. Slivers of dark blue rested on the horizon, and a full moon followed him all the way to the fallen tree that bridged the water. A robin hopped in the shadows, along a branch. Here, on the bank, Megs sat down, too afraid to go further.

Placing his feet carefully, he walked halfway across the fallen tree and sat down on its smooth trunk. His legs dangled over metallic waters, which churned and shone beneath him.

Until a few minutes ago, his whole life had been mapped out before him. Nothing stood in his way, apart from a few pointless years at school. He was going to work the farm like his father, grandfather and great-grandfather before him. He would spend all his time sheep-dipping, herding, shearing, mending fences, fixing engines. Looking after the land and driving the tractor and digger and quad bike in all weathers. Megs, only a puppy now, would become a highly trained sheepdog, zipping this way and that, to keep the sheep in line. And he would breed from her and her pups until he was as old as Gramp.

But now, none of that was going to happen. Mum would lose her jam business, Tommo wouldn't grow up on the farm and Dad and Gramp would have to leave the place they'd lived in all their lives. And Dylan could forget about building a treehouse with his friends. The map had been wiped clean.

Dylan pressed his newly sharpened pencil into the bottom of the poster until it made a neat hole. He leaned against the wall, his right hand hidden by his left arm, so the teacher couldn't see what he was doing.

It was a stupid poster anyway. Arrows showed evaporation from lakes and streams forming clouds which blew over oceans and continents to hilltops and then dropped the rain back into mountain streams again. As if anyone needed to go to school to be taught that – you could see it with your own eyes, if you weren't stuck in a smelly classroom.

If you just got off your backside, as Gramp would say, and followed the river upstream, through the woods, past the boggy uplands, on and on and up to the top of the hill at the farm's northern boundary, you'd see exactly what the clouds were doing. Sometimes, when he had too much energy boiling around inside him, Dylan went up there on his own to feel the wind on his neck and nothing but the sky above him.

The smell in the Geography classroom was a mixture of armpits, socks and sharp chemical cleaning liquids. Mrs Hughes' voice droned, bee-like, in his brain, urging them to study hard now that they had started secondary school.

'Young man! Are you listening?'

Dylan jolted in his seat. Mrs Hughes was talking to him.

'After the school trip to Harlech over half-term you will be expected to hand in your Geography project. It is a chance to expand your mind.'

He glared at her and made another hole with his pencil.

She had one pair of glasses in the normal place, on her

nose, and another pair on her head, just visible in her hair. It was springy, blonde hair, like coils of wool. Like sheep's wool, in fact, just before shearing, with long shaggy bits dangling below her ears. A pen poked out from behind one ear. There were probably several more pens and pencils hiding in that hair. Dylan wouldn't be surprised if there was a ruler and a few rubbers in there as well. She probably didn't even need a handbag.

Last night, when everyone was asleep, he had googled BlueBird to find out what dad meant by the see-ee-oh. Dylan clicked on 'Our People'. At the top it said Mustafa Shadid, Chief Executive Officer. Oh, thought Dylan, CEO.

A picture of a man with dark skin and short dark curly hair filled the screen. He had a wide smile and looked like the kind of man you could talk to. If Dylan could just find him – where? Dylan clicked on the contacts page and found offices all over world except the UK. That was the end of that, then.

Dylan flicked down the rest of the photos in 'Our People'. They all looked perfectly nice. Did he really think he would find a cartoon baddie among them, with rotting teeth, a grey face and evil red eyes? Then Dylan got a shock. Way down at the bottom of the list, a face he knew glared out at him. Floyd's face.

It wasn't Floyd of course. It was much older for a start, with a wild, staring expression, whereas Floyd always looked cold and serious. He checked the name. Mac Adams, it said. Floyd's dad. Floyd had said he worked abroad, and here he was, working for the same company that had just bought their farm. The job description said Consultant Conservationist, whatever that meant. One of his jobs had been in Scotland, where he had surveyed aquatic plants and mosses in rivers and lochs. It also said he had sampled and identified earthworms. Sampled? Didn't that mean he ate them? Mum sent samples of jam to people. If he ate worms, he might not be the sort of dad who would be much help.

Here he was, caged, listening to his teacher waffling on with Floyd sitting in another classroom only a few feet away. If she thought he was going to waste any time on her project, she had another think coming.

'The project title is Human Impact on the Environment. You can choose anything that human beings have done, past or present. Assess whether it is a good or bad impact, or a mixture of both.'

Dylan almost growled. She looked like one of those people who spent all their free time reading instead of going outside and doing any of the things in her books. Like actually going up a tree. Or making a huge bike track with jumps, or building a treehouse you could sleep in. Or trudging off in the rain through gorse and bracken and over mossy mounds to the far edges of the farm with a dog to rescue a sheep some tourist had said was stuck in a fence.

Dylan hadn't slept much. He had spent every waking second wracking his brains to work out how they could get the farm back. He wasn't any good at schoolwork and he had never got the hang of being polite, but – and it wasn't boasting if you only said it to yourself – he was pretty good at making things happen.

He had plenty of ideas. Some were too big: computer hacking to change the sale, kidnapping the CEO, tying himself to the rope swing and refusing to leave. And some were too soft: taking all the road signs to his village away, using the digger like a tank to stop BlueBird from entering the village, setting up a petition. But he hadn't come up with anything you could call a real plan. And how was he supposed to think with his teacher droning on and on?'

'I'd like to see the human element,' she continued, 'talk to people involved if you can. Sometimes the essays that win are the ones that show how passionate the writer is. So look for something you really care about.'

Dylan sighed. She was smiling now and he could tell immediately that she had something granny-ish – like elderflower – running in her veins. To be fair, she probably had no idea how much she was torturing him.

Deep inside, a nasty dark thought hunkered down, waiting for the right moment. That thought was: it was impossible. Global companies didn't sell farms back because some kid wanted them to. Dylan shoved the thought roughly aside.

He had to go and see Floyd after school and get his dad's email address. Gramp would call it clutching at straws. But it was better than doing nothing.

TWO

That evening after tea, Dylan picked Megs up and pressed his face into the soft fur on the back of her neck so Tommo couldn't see his expression. Matt and the twins, Aled and Rob, would be waiting for them, sitting on the fallen tree.

'Go to the river without me,' he told Tommo. 'I'm not coming.'

'What about the treehouse?' Tommo asked. 'I thought we were gonna...'

'I said, go!' Dylan snapped.

Tommo gave him a funny look and opened his mouth, but Dylan scowled and left the kitchen. He could just about hide his feelings from Tommo, but not from Matt. Matt would demand to know what was wrong and Dylan knew he couldn't make something up.

When Dylan was four, he'd been digging a tunnel in the sandpit in the village playground when, deep underground, his fingers had met more fingers. He had looked up to see an astonished freckled face. They had both burst out laughing and been best friends ever since. The thought of seeing Matt this evening, knowing that he, Dylan, might have to leave the village forever, was unbearable.

Megs trotted happily beside Dylan on the way to Floyd's house. Closing the garden gate behind him, he walked straight past the front door and onto the grass. He threw a small pebble up so it tapped on Floyd's bedroom window. No response. He tried again. On the third try, a head popped out of the window.

'Come down, will you?' Dylan hissed. 'I need to ask you something.'

'It's too late. I'll see you tomorrow.' The head popped back in again.

'It's about your dad.'

Floyd's head came out again, glowering, and then disappeared. Footsteps pounded down the stairs. A moment later the front door opened.

'Shut up about my dad. It'll upset my mum.' Floyd marched off towards the garden shed, his hands thrust deep into his pockets, the ice in his veins as cold and hard as when he first came to the village.

Being able to see what flowed in people's veins wasn't something Dylan had ever mentioned to anyone.

Whenever he tried to put it into words, it sounded silly. But for as long as he could remember, he had been able to see right inside people. Not what they wanted you to see, but what made them who they really were. And not see it, exactly, but feel it deep in his bones.

Mum, for instance, had pure strawberry juice running in her veins. Everyone should be able to see that. That's why she was so round and huggable and quite red in the face. Dad usually had exactly the right amount of engine oil running through him – he must have absorbed it through his fingers, that's why he was so good at fixing things. Matt had marmite – sensible, everyday marmite – in his veins, which made sense because he was great if he liked you, awful if he didn't. The twins had grown so tall, so fast, that it was hard to be sure – something like the spangly, soapy water for blowing bubbles in Rob, and something denser, almost like floppy spaghetti, in Aled. And Tommo – Tommo was a jelly bean, everyone liked him and old ladies always said he was sweet.

Dylan's own blood usually surged in bursts, boiling and popping, which was why it was so hard to sit in a classroom doing nothing instead of getting on with stuff.

But he had never met anyone like Floyd. At the beginning of the summer, Dylan had seen something straight off about Floyd. Something so cold it would take the skin off your fingers if you touched it. Hard, sharp. Icicles, needles, splinters of glass. Whatever was in his veins had frozen over. By the end of the summer, when

Floyd told Dylan about his brother, they made their peace and Dylan had seen Floyd's veins begin to creak and move with a pale blue liquid. Now, just a few days later, they had frosted again.

Floyd flung the shed door open and Dylan followed. Inside, it was practically empty. Dylan's dad's workshop was crammed with tools: saws, hammers, garden spades, rakes, crusty gardening gloves, chisels and plenty of shapes you couldn't name. This garden shed had nothing but a lawnmower and two bikes, one covered in mud and a smaller one as clean as if it had come out of the shop two minutes before. Joe's bike.

What none of the others knew was that Floyd had a younger brother, Joe, who he hadn't seen for six months. After Floyd's dad took a job in Brazil, he had asked Floyd's mum if he could take Joe with him for the Easter holidays. Trouble was, they didn't come back. Floyd and his mum didn't tell anyone when they came to live in the village, and even Dylan wasn't supposed to know.

Floyd waited for Dylan to close the door. He glared at Dylan.

'What do you want?' he demanded, as if he thought Dylan had come to pick a fight.

As Dylan looked at Floyd's angry, tight face, it occurred to him that he didn't really have any idea of who Floyd would be if his brother wasn't away in another country. But that didn't make it any easier to be with him.

'Your dad still works for that stupid face-cream

company, BlueBird, right?' He hadn't meant to be rude, it just came out that way.

'It's not a stupid face-cream company. It's a top pharmaceutical company.'

'Farmer-suit-ical? That's a joke.'

'No, P-H. Like pharmacy. A chemists. You know, they make medicines. Or drugs, my dad calls them. That's the American word, anyway. Dad says BlueBird is the best drugs company in the world, discovering amazing new medicines from natural sources. His job is making sure it's eco-friendly and…'

'Bluebird's just bought our farm, Floyd, so you can cut the big sell.'

'Bought – your farm?' Floyd's cold eyes met Dylan's.

'Yeah. Just when we were about to.'

Floyd played with Megs' ear. 'Does that mean … you'll have to leave? The village?'

Dylan swallowed.

'Not if I can fix things,' he said. It sounded ridiculous. He stood a little straighter. 'I need to talk to your dad. Can you give me his email? I just need to explain something and everything will go back to normal.'

Floyd's face paled and his whole body stiffened.

'No.'

'No? Wha…?'

'You can't talk to him. I can't talk to him. We've lost touch with them. The last time I heard from Joe was nine days ago. He sounded scared.'

'Scared of your dad?'

Floyd's jaw clenched and he breathed in deeply. 'I wouldn't have said anyone could be scared of my dad, but yes.' He looked up at the ceiling. 'If you must know, Joe said Dad had started drawing on the walls, sticking bits of paper all over them. Shouting down the phone at strangers. Ranting about a second project. I mean, he always talked to himself, but it sounds like he's got worse. Then Joe went silent. No emails, no Skype calls, not even a text.'

For the first moment in twenty-four hours Dylan stopped thinking about the farm.

'What did your mum say?'

'I didn't tell her. It would make her…' Floyd stopped and gazed out of the window. 'She says her whole body aches, she misses Joe so much. I can hear her crying at night.'

'And the judge? Wasn't a judge going to do something about it?'

'Dad hasn't answered his letter. It might take months.' Whatever was holding Floyd up like a plank, collapsed. He slid down to the wooden floor and studied it.

'If I could just talk to Dad, I could get him to send Joe home.'

Dylan also slid down and pulled a splinter out of the floorboards.

'Yeah, right. Like if I could just talk to the CEO – or anyone – at BlueBird. You know, go to one of the offices or wherever he…'

'There's a big office in Salvador, Brazil, where my dad is.'

Dylan stuck his splinter into a small hole and dug some sawdust out.

'So if we could just nip over to Brazil…'

'Yeah, if we could … teleport over there.'

'Yup,' Dylan said. 'Like just hop over all that sea.'

'Five thousand five hundred and sixty eight miles.'

'You actually know that?'

'I know a lot about Brazil,' Floyd said. 'But it doesn't do any good. It's impossible to get there. We're stuck in this tiny village, miles from anywhere. We couldn't even get to Machynlleth, let alone an airport.'

Five thousand, five hundred and sixty-eight miles between Dylan and a big office with loads of people who worked at BlueBird. And someone who had the power to say, 'Oh, OK, we didn't know you wanted to buy your farm. That's fine, we'll buy the one in the next village, then. You can have yours back. Done deal.' And Floyd's dad lived there.

Dylan traced around a knot of wood in the floor with the splinter. The knot was like a boulder in the river, a large lump that all the lines had to swerve around. It made him think of the swirls and eddies and white spray when the water hit a rock. Nothing stopped the river. He knew that from trying to dam it. If there was something in the way, the river just swirled round it, or leaked under it, or built up so much pressure behind the obstacle that eventually it poured over it. The river always found a way.

Floyd was wrong about one thing, though. Getting to Machynlleth would be easy. Dylan pictured the route to town. Up to the main road, turn left, go past the kennels and cattery, round the roundabout. On and on. You could easily cycle it.

'You could get to Machynlleth,' he said. 'It'd take about an hour on a bike. And you could get to an airport from there by train. Birmingham, for instance.'

Floyd grunted.

'But you couldn't go without a passport, of course,' Dylan said. He had one, they'd all got them to go to France by ferry last year and he was very proud of it. But Floyd might not have one.

'Oh, I've got a passport,' Floyd said, as if it was nothing.

'But it would cost zillions to fly to Brazil.'

Floyd dug his splinter into the crack between floorboards and flipped out a spray of sawdust.

'My grandpa gives me a cheque every Christmas and it just goes into my bank account. I don't care about the money, I just want Joe back.'

'You have a bank account?'

'Yeah. You can get one when you're eleven. Mum opened it for me.'

'With a card 'n' all? The sort you can buy things online with?'

Floyd nodded.

'I've got some money left over from the summer,' Dylan said. 'And I could earn more.'

Dylan dropped his splinter and looked straight at Floyd. His chest and brain were getting hot. But Floyd was shaking his head.

'It's not possible,' Floyd said.

Dylan's chest churned with life. It wouldn't only be possible – it would be easy. He sprang to his feet, suddenly desperate for action.

'What's stopping us? We've got money and passports. Why don't we just buy the tickets?' It was all so clear. They would stay at Floyd's dad's place and he, Dylan, could go to BlueBird's office the next day and explain to someone what had happened and tell them about the Evans' farm. He might not find the CEO, but he would find someone. They would definitely listen to a kid who had travelled all the way from Wales. Grown-ups were soft like that.

'Let's go online – right now – let's just see how much it is, how long it takes, all that,' he said. How could Floyd just sit there? 'Where is BlueBird and Salvador exactly, anyway?' Was Dylan imagining it, or was the ice in Floyd's veins beginning to creak and move?

'On the coast. South of the equator,' Floyd said slowly. He wasn't smiling, he wasn't excited yet, like Dylan was.

The only things Dylan knew about Brazil were that it was the size of Europe and they played football the whole time. And now, that it was five thousand, five hundred and sixty eight miles away.

'Other side of the world, then,' breathed Dylan.

The boys crept past Floyd's mum as she watched a survival programme on TV about eating caterpillars in the jungle. On the kitchen computer they googled flights. At first they got El Salvador instead, a country south of Mexico. Then they realised their mistake and the right flights, for Salvador, a city in Brazil, came up. The flight took sixteen hours, with a stop in Lisbon. They put in their ages to see what the price would be. Adults: 0, Young Adults: 2. A red sign flashed up: young adults between the ages of 11 and 15 travelling alone must have a signed letter of authorisation from a family member, it said.

'See. I told you it was impossible,' Floyd said, sitting back in the chair, defeated.

'You can't just give up,' Dylan said. 'We have to work out how to get round it, that's all. We could forge a signature?'

'I tried copying mum's once on a sick note,' Floyd said. 'You can tell it's not a grown-up's writing. Maybe you could get your dad to sign it.'

'He doesn't know I know. And I heard him say he can't even talk about it yet. Maybe we could find an adult who was busy, who wouldn't really look at it.'

'Yeah, right. Have to be a seriously irresponsible adult,' said Floyd.

A seriously irresponsible adult.

'The sort that doesn't pay his bills,' Dylan said, slowly. 'The sort that has vices. Like gambling. The sort that leaves his plates and beer cans by the TV until he runs out and has to wash up because he hasn't any left.'

'Yeah, that's exactly the sort of adult,' said Floyd, dully, as if there was no hope of finding one like that.

As if there wasn't one who fitted that description in their very village.

THREE

Gramp's house was only up the lane from Dylan's house, but it looked completely different. Bins overflowed by the back door and two of the window panes had been replaced with plastic sheeting. A dump, his parents called it, and although for years Dylan couldn't see what they meant, recently he had noticed that it was a bit messy. The boys tiptoed up to Gramp's door, careful to step around a wheel-less wheelbarrow full of broken stuff: a toaster, a kettle without a lid, a saucepan with a hole in the bottom.

'Look in through here,' whispered Dylan, waving at Floyd to peer in through one of the real windows.

'Blimey,' Floyd said. Dylan couldn't tell whether he was impressed or appalled.

The sink was full of dirty dishes, and a large saucepan, filled with more plates and bowls, stood on the kitchen table. Three plates were on the floor and Bella, Gramp's old sheepdog, was licking one of them, chasing it around. Stacks of magazines, all with horses on the front, balanced on each stool.

Dylan was about to knock when Floyd grabbed on to his arm.

'Is this his normal sort of mess?'

'Yup.'

'And you really think he'll sign a form – maybe several – without even looking at it?'

Dylan thought about it. 'I'll eat my trousers if he looks at it.'

'Who's there?' Gramp called out. The front door opened and Gramp, dressed in pyjama bottoms and a holey jumper stood in the doorway, looking this way and that. His white hair stood up on end as if he had just had an electric shock and his bushy white eyebrows moved up and down and left and right as if they were reacting to completely different things. He had a pen stuck above his left ear.

'Hi Gramp, this is Floyd. We just came to say hello.'

'Champion idea. Come in. I'll knock up some pancakes and we'll have a feast.'

At that moment, Dylan's mother's voice rang out 'Dylan! Where are you? School tomorrow. Come in now!'

The boys hesitated on the doorstep.

'Take no notice,' Gramp said. 'You can catch up on sleep in lessons if you're gonna be stuck in some hummin' classroom all day. Silly waste of time if you ask me. Floyd, come in. I've heard a lot about you. Welcome to our part of Wales, boy. You're from Cardiff, isn't it?'

The boys followed Gramp into his cottage. There was a strange sweet smell, like candyfloss, but burnt.

'Bin' making toffee,' said Gramp. 'Only I forgot about it and it's gone a bit black. Suck it. It'll take your teeth out if you chew it.' He handed them what looked like a broken piece of black glass.

'Great toffee,' Floyd mumbled, sucking his enormous piece.

Gramp must have had some sort of cooking disaster, because yellow splats covered part of the wall. It had gone hard and stuck in yellow droplets, like something in the Tabernacle art gallery.

'What happened to your wall, Gramp?'

'Looks good, eh? Tripped over Bella and the custard went everywhere. By the time I got around to clearing it up it was all dry, and I thought to myself, John, you could do worse than to leave it right there. You could pay a lot to have that sort of thing on your wall. I'll fix up a pancake then, shall I?'

'Gramp, we'd better not stay. Mum'll be cross otherwise.'

As they left, Gramp tore off two strips from a magazine, wrapped a piece of toffee in each one, and handed them out. After waving goodbye, Dylan ran back, pulling a piece of paper out of his pocket.

'Gramp, could you just sign this for me? I need it for tomorrow. It's to say I couldn't get all my homework done tonight.'

The old man grinned at him, turned Dylan round and placed the piece of paper on his upper back. Dylan held his breath and glanced at Floyd, who was staring intently at the old man. Gramp pulled the pen from behind his ear and, without a moment's hesitation, scrawled a signature and handed the paper back.

'Homework. Never did understand all that fuss and bother. As if spending all day long in school isn't bad enough. Hell on wheels, that is. 'Scruciating. All that French and Physics and stuff. As if that's going to be any help when you're on a tractor in the driving rain looking for a lost lamb.'

That last bit – the fact that Dylan might never be on a tractor in the driving rain, looking for a lost lamb – knocked the wind out of Dylan's guts for a moment. He managed a small smile and a few nods.

'G'night, Gramp,' he said.

Dylan and Floyd marched side by side, not daring to look at each other until they were out of sight of Gramp's cottage.

'He's great!' Floyd said. 'It was easy!' Floyd turned and rested his back against the wall. His face was all lit up. 'Maybe we really could do it. Get to Salvador, take the metro to Dad's, see Joe. Bring him home.' His voice was full of wonder and hope. 'Joe could be here, with me, playing in our garden. He could meet Tommo. In a couple of weeks, it could all be over.' He gave a huge grin and held a palm up to high five Dylan.

FOUR

The next morning, in the rush of bodies entering the school, Dylan felt a tap on his shoulder. He turned to see Floyd behind him.

'We need a list of problems,' muttered Floyd, once he was close enough.

'I thought we solved them all last night,' said Dylan, as the bunch of people around him spread out on the other side of the entrance doors. Matt was ahead of them in the corridor, hanging back, waiting for them.

'Change the subject,' whispered Floyd. 'Hi Matt, how's it going?' He called out.

'Cool.' Matt let them catch up with him and walked alongside them. When they stopped, he stopped. 'What's up? You coming in to class?'

'Er, yeah, in a bit. I'll catch you up, Matt,' Dylan said.

'Oh. Fine.'

Matt reached the end of the corridor and disappeared. He didn't do his usual jokey turnaround and shoot routine.

'He knows we're leaving him out of something, Floyd.'

'Well, we can't tell him. We can't tell anyone. Come over to my house tonight and we'll go through everything.'

In History, Dylan went to sit next to Matt. Dylan kept talking to him and being told off and talking to him again, and by the end, Matt was as easy and jokey as ever. But at lunch break Floyd came up to them both and made it obvious he only wanted to speak to Dylan, and Matt walked off with his brick wall face on.

On the way home, Matt didn't leave any room for Dylan to sit next to him on the bus, and he jumped off too quickly for Dylan to catch up.

'Have you got homework?' asked his mum.

'Some,' said Dylan. 'Some sums, in fact.'

'That's a rubbish pun, Dyl,' she said.

'I know.'

'Is something the matter?'

'No,' he said, and went to his bedroom.

When he had had a go at some of his homework and had tea, he walked down the hill to the Old Vicarage where Floyd lived. He passed Matt's house on the way. As he looked in at the window and saw Matt turn his head away, Dylan seemed to see the next few days play out like a film in front of his eyes.

He and Floyd would have more and more things to talk about and Matt would be more and more left out. Even if they tried to have secret meetings, Matt would know something was up. And you couldn't mess about with Matt. You couldn't stop being friends for few weeks, then expect to be friends again. He just wasn't like that.

Dylan's plans for going to Brazil shrivelled. If Matt wasn't talking to him, there wouldn't be any point in saving the farm. It wasn't just life on the farm he wanted. It was bigger than that. It was life here in this village, with his friends, that was just as important. He would never, ever have friends like these ones again. Floyd couldn't be expected to understand; he'd only come to the village a couple of months ago.

Dylan managed to drag himself along for the remaining paces to Floyd's house, but by the time he reached it, he came to a full stop. He couldn't ring the bell. He couldn't go through with a plan as huge as this without telling Matt. Going to Brazil with Floyd was his one chance to save the whole farm. But what would be the point of getting the farm back if Matt wasn't speaking to him? He stared at the bell.

As he stood, trapped with an impossible choice, the door opened.

'Why are you standing there? I saw you from my bedroom window. You've been there for ten minutes.'

'Floyd, we're gonna have to tell Matt.'

'What? No, this has to be a secret.'

'Won't we need a back-up team here at home? You know, to put our mothers off the track or something?'

'What if he wants to come too?'

'I don't know, but we still have to tell him. We can't just let him think we don't like him.'

'We can't risk it. I can't lose the chance of getting Joe back because someone tells their mum.'

It had seemed such a good plan: now Dylan would have to think up another. A quick gust of wind and the sharp fresh smell it brought told him rain would come soon. He had to say it.

'Then I can't come with you, Floyd. I can't have a secret from Matt. He's not stupid. I don't even want to talk about it any more.' Dylan turned away, and felt a hand on his arm.

'No, wait. OK. So we tell Matt.'

'And the others.'

'What?'

'Tommo. And Aled and Rob.'

'You must be kidding. This isn't a game. You can't tell everyone just to be nice.'

'It's the only way I can come, Floyd. And we have to pretend it's only to get Joe. We can't mention my farm or BlueBird. I can't tell people about that before my dad does.'

'What if they tell their parents? What about Tommo? He's too young to keep a secret.'

'Tommo won't say a word. I can make sure of that.'

A long low groan escaped Floyd. 'And this is the only way you'll come?'

Dylan didn't answer.

'OK then. They just better not tell their parents.'

A huge grin spread over Dylan's face and he raced back up to Matt's house and banged on the door.

Matt's mother opened it.

'Hi. Can Matt come out?'

'He says he's got too much homework, Dylan,' she said, looking embarrassed.

'It's … it's about homework. I really need to talk to him. Please ask him just to come to the door.'

Matt came to the door and gazed across the road to the village hall, as if Dylan was invisible.

'Matt, can you come to Floyd's house now? We need to tell you something.'

Matt shrugged. 'Can't you tell me here?'

'No. And bring Rob and Aled. I'm getting Tommo.'

In Floyd's bedroom, a map of Brazil covered one wall, with one red pin stuck on the word Salvador. Otherwise the room was bare. Rob stood on one leg by the window. Matt, Aled and Tommo sat on the bed. These were Dylan's people – the ones he was meant to be with and it hurt to think that one day he and Tommo might be missing from this group.

Once Tommo had stopped fidgeting, Dylan began.

'We've got a plan,' he said.

'We? You or Floyd?' asked Aled.

'Er, Floyd,' said Dylan.

'Oh good. If it was you, it would be dangerous, nearly impossible and we would all have to take part.'

Dylan and Floyd looked at each other.

'We're going to get Joe,' Floyd said.

'Who's Joe?'

'My brother and he's in Brazil.'

'What?' Came four voices at once.

'Let me explain,' said Dylan. 'Floyd has a younger brother who lives in Brazil with his dad. Only he's supposed to live here with Floyd and his mum. And they've both gone silent. So we're going to get him, Floyd and me. We're going to Brazil to bring him back.'

'This is a joke, right?' Matt said, getting up off the bed.

'No, wait, Matt, sit down. This isn't a joke. We mean it. We've got the money and passports. It's what we've been talking about at school. We've found flights. We're working it all out.' The bit about the money wasn't quite true yet, but Dylan would think about that later.

There was a long silence while Matt, Aled, Rob and Tommo all looked from Dylan's face to Floyd's, and back again, like people watching tennis.

'So why are you telling us?' Matt said eventually.

'We need your help.'

'Have you lost your minds?' Aled said. 'OK.' He stuck his fingers out and started ticking them off. 'One, how are the aeroplane people going to let you just come and go as if you're adults? Two, how do you get from Salvador airport to your dad's house? Three, how is your dad just going to let Joe go? Four, oh, this is mental.'

'A list! That's exactly what we need! Then we can start sorting things out.'

'I thought you'd want to come,' said Floyd, limply.

'Want to come?' Aled snorted. 'I'll be impressed if you get as far as Birmingham. And what about your mums when they find out you've disappeared? They'll go ballistic. Then they'll start crying. Then they'll send your photo to the papers.'

'There are headhunters in Brazil. You might get scalped.' Rob said.

Floyd and Dylan went quiet. Dylan glanced at Matt, whose face was screwed up in a frown with a scrunched mouth.

'Perhaps we could say we were staying at someone else's house?' said Dylan.

'For a week?'

'I only need three days,' said Floyd.

'Haven't you heard of jetlag?' asked Aled. 'Missing a plane? Getting on the wrong plane?'

'That's if the piranhas don't get you, of course,' added Rob. He shuddered. 'Nibble, nibble, nibble.'

'Hey!' Matt's eyes lit up and he leapt off the bed.

'What?' asked Dylan and Floyd.

'How about you go when the geography trip is on? At

half-term? So your parents know you're away, but you go to Brazil instead?'

'Genius!' cried Dylan.

'What about your project for the Geography competition? How will you get that done if you're flying all over the place all week?' Aled said.

Dylan shrugged. 'Wasn't planning on doing that anyway.'

'You can't just not do it, Dyl.'

'Can. Watch me. I'll print off some pages, stick them in a big puddle and drive over them with the digger. Then I'll hand it in.'

'Half term's not until October,' said Floyd. 'I can't wait that long.'

'Gives us time to plan. And for me to do some more jobs,' said Dylan. 'Matt's right, half-term is perfect. And another thing. We need a back-up team here at home. Matt – you'll be on the Geography trip, so you can tell us what we need to know to sound convincing about it.'

'Maybe you're right,' Floyd's shoulders slumped. 'I thought we'd go next week.'

'I'll help,' said Tommo in a small voice. 'But how can I help you in Brazil when I'm here at home?'

'I need you to look after Megs, OK? Aled? Rob? Will you help?'

Rob sighed. 'Yes, yes, I'll help. I'm a bit scared of going on the geography trip to Harlech to be honest. But, OK.'

'Aled?'

'Sure I'll help. But you'll get into real trouble and waste loads of money,' said Aled in a gloomy voice. 'Unless you actually get there, in which case you'll get lost and probably murdered in Brazil. And you want us to say we knew and thought it was a good idea?'

There was a silence.

'Yes,' said Dylan, his heart thumping. What Aled said didn't sound impossible. But they had to try, didn't they? If they succeeded, and Dylan managed to get someone at BlueBird to understand, everyone would be happy, Dad, Mum, Floyd and his mum. Tommo would have Joe, someone his own age in the village. And he, Dylan, would be back to Plan A: sitting on the fallen tree planning the tree house with all his mates. Spending evenings and weekends nailing planks together, hammering away until they had a den up in the branches. With his whole life on the farm, here in this village with all his mates, spread out before him.

'We won't get lost,' he said. 'We'll research it really well, won't we? We'll go straight to Floyd's dad's house and straight back to the airport. Simples.'

'Murdered?' said Tommo.

'Don't listen to him, Tommo.'

FIVE

For the next five weeks the boys were on Floyd's laptop, comparing flight prices, practising filling in forms, looking up Google Earth to find out ways of getting from Salvador airport to Mac Adams's flat. They printed off the Form of Indemnity for Unaccompanied Young Passengers – twice – and Gramp signed without even looking at them, with his big, loose, unmistakeably adult signature.

Matt did some research and told them they'd better take mosquito spray, Aled found out they spoke Portuguese in Brazil, which meant they probably wouldn't even be able to find the exit from the airport; and Rob suggested they stop at the art gallery in Birmingham if they had time, because the marble staircases and pink walls and all the paintings were something else. Tommo jumped up and down quite a bit.

In his pyjamas one night, when his mum and dad were watching a police programme they never missed a single minute of, Dylan printed the map of Salvador and drew a route from Floyd's dad's address to the BlueBird office. If Mac Adams wasn't helpful, he would walk there. Then he deleted his history on the computer and closed it all down.

Dylan did odd jobs, cleaning cars to raise money. Gramp gave him a bit, too, when he told him he was working on an important project.

'Here y'are, lad. You take it. Been keeping this for the electric, but if you've got a plan, it'll be a good'un.'

Dylan counted. It was generous, but it wasn't enough. Then, during Maths one day, a strong wind shook the trees, tussled with them for their golden leaves. The wind won and the leaves drifted across the classroom window in their hundreds. While the rest of the class was working on dividing and multiplying by negative numbers, Dylan calculated how long it would take to fill a bag with leaves, how much he could charge for each bag and how many houses in the village would give him work.

One night, from Tommo's bunk there came a whisper.

'Dylan, why did Aled say you might get murdered?'

'Because he doesn't like anything new or strange.'

'Not because Brazil really is dangerous?'

'How much do you think Aled knows about Brazil? All he knows is that it's different and a long way away. I bet it isn't all that different anyway. Gramp says everywhere's pretty much the same. People do the same things all over the world. He says there's nothing better than your own home and farm, so not to waste your time looking for it. I bet there are families there just like ours. Bet there are lots of houses with two brothers sharing a bedroom telling each other funny stories and stuff like that. Probably even one exactly like ours, with a bunkbed each so they can have friends round.'

Tommo made funny noises as he snuggled in his bed.

'Thought so. Thought that would be it,' came a drowsy voice.

SIX

'Mum, can you take Matt and Floyd and me to school really early for the Geography trip? And not wait around?'

'You mean you're ashamed of me?'

'Don't be daft, Mum. I just don't want to be one of those baby kids whose mums keep hugging them and stuff, as if they'll never see them again. It's only five days. You can come to school with me any other time.'

Dylan pulled a rucksack down from the top of the cupboard. He threw in shorts, crocs and three T-shirts. That should be enough. When his mum came to say goodnight, she looked at what he'd packed and laughed.

'That's optimistic,' she said. 'You can throw all that stuff out. You'll need your waterproofs, a thick fleece and some walking boots. It's not summer anymore, you know.' She shook her head. 'You're still a kid, even if you can drive a tractor.'

When the door clicked closed behind her, Tommo spoke.

'Dylan, how will I talk to you? I haven't got a phone or email. How can I let you know what's happening here?'

Dylan climbed up his steps onto his bunk and glanced over at Tommo. He couldn't believe he, Dylan, had ever been as young as that.

'My phone won't work in Brazil, it's too rubbish. But Floyd's will. If I need to tell you anything I'll use Floyd's phone to ring Gramp, OK, and Gramp will come and find you.'

'Oh, OK.'

'And I need you to take Megs to the tree every day, so she stops being scared of it. You don't have to put her on it, just take her to play a bit nearer it each day.'

Tommo's face lit up and he nodded.

Dylan wondered how he'd feel if Dad had taken Tommo off to the other side of the world for several months. Tommo could be pretty annoying, but Dylan couldn't imagine not having him around.

At Loisin Lush in town, Dylan went in with his last pound. Jars of sweets of every single kind you could think of – and some you couldn't – lined the wall behind the cash desk. He spent it all on a pink stripy paper bag of jelly beans. The night before the Geography trip he gave it to Tommo.

'Every time you think you're going to tell Mum about my trip, or any time you miss me, eat one of these, OK? And remember it'll all be fine and I'll be back at the end of the week. I'm going to say goodbye now because Mum'll think it's weird if we're doing some sort of heavy goodbye scene when I'm just going on a school trip. OK? So give me a hug, squid-face.'

Tommo looked up at Dylan with big eyes.

'You're so brave, Dyl,' he said. 'If you were stuck in Brazil, I'm not sure I would be brave enough to come and get you.' His lower lip trembled. 'I've been thinking about it. I'm really sorry, Dyl. I think I could chop off my finger if it would bring you back, with Daddy's axe, but I just don't think I could go to Brazil without Mum or Dad.' Tommo looked on the brink of tears.

Dylan squeezed Tommo's shoulders.

'Course not. That's the way it is. But if you were my age and you had a little brother like you, stuck somewhere, you would be able to. And don't you dare go anywhere near Dad's axe. Ever. OK?'

Tommo nodded and wiped his eyes.

'Thanks for the jelly beans,' he said.

SEVEN

Dylan's mum was ready, as promised, when the day was still only a red streak on the horizon, under a dark sky. She dropped them off at the school twenty minutes before anyone else turned up. She was good like that. Not one of those needy mums who glued themselves to you. Dylan gave Megs one last hug and got his ear licked. As he watched his mother's curly head disappearing round the corner, it occurred to him that if Aled was right, and something awful happened, he might never see her again. He swallowed. It was stupid to think like that. He was only going to Floyd's dad's place.

There was one thing he needed to do before they left for the train station.

'Matt, Floyd, listen,' he said. He took a printed letter out of his rucksack and read it out.

Dear Mrs Hughes, it said

I'm afraid Dylan and Floyd won't be coming on the Geography trip after all. They have both been up all night puking their guts out so I think there's something going round and the last thing you need is a whole school trip of puking children.

Sorry about that. I know the cost of the trip can't be refunded now, but it can't be helped.

Illegible Scrawl

'Puking their guts out? What did you put that for? Your mum would never say that. She'd say, "vomiting", or "being ill", or something. This is rubbish!' Matt said.

'I thought it was pretty good,' said Dylan. 'I could have written "spewing" or "barfing" or "chundering".'

'"Regurgitating" would have been worse. That would have seemed like someone trying to sound grown-up,' said Floyd.

'Or throwing up. Retching or heaving or chucking up. Or upchucking.'

'My dad calls it doing the technicolour yawn,' said Matt. 'He's got lots of words for it. "Tossing one's cookies", that's another one. Oh, and "praying to the porcelain god".'

'How does that mean being sick?' asked Dylan.

'Haven't a clue.'

'Can you two shut up?' Floyd said. 'There's nothing we can do about it now anyway. He'll just think your mum's nuts, Dylan. Let's go or some other kids will get here and see us.'

'Matt, remember to tell us loads of stuff about the trip, OK? So we can sound convincing. Like, details – what you eat, what group you're in for sleeping, all that kind of thing.'

Matt banged Dylan on the back.

'Bye, mate. Bye, Floyd. Bring me back something.'

Dylan and Floyd pulled their hoodies up and walked out of the school car park towards town. At the train station, they huddled at the very end of the platform, diving into the last carriage as soon a the train came.

When the ticket collector came they showed him the tickets they had bought a week before.

'Half term, eh? Where are you two rapscallions off to?'

'Seeing, er, his family,' said Dylan.

'Ah. All the way to Birmingham on your own? That's bold.'

'Er, yessir.'

'That's the furthest I've ever been and I only got off once. One visit was enough for me. Nasty, noisy things, cities are. Much better off here in the hills. What've they got that we haven't, anyway?'

'The Science Museum is pretty cool,' said Floyd. 'Aston Villa football stadium. And I'm told the art gallery is worth a visit.'

The conductor looked baffled. 'That's just a bunch of bother, that is.' He walked off, shaking his head.

The train shot on, taking the boys further and further

away from home. Fields and bare trees shot past, with calm scenes of cows and sheep munching on grass. Everyone said Wales was so green, but they must have sheep in Brazil, Dylan thought, so what did all their livestock eat if it wasn't green?

Eventually though, the fields disappeared and endless back gardens zipped past the train, all, Dylan thought, belonging to families he would never know.

Birmingham International was huge. Dylan didn't notice exactly where the train station ended and the airport began, he just realised they were in it. It was nearly as big as the farm, but all covered over in shiny floors and high ceilings and massive adverts and not an animal anywhere. There probably wasn't even a single flea living in the whole space.

'We need Flight TAP 331,' said Floyd. They scanned the boards above all the queues of people. 'There it is.' Without a word, both boys raced off towards the TAP airline check-in desk and joined the queue. They shuffled their bags along, looking at the ground. There was nothing to say. They had checked every website and they all said it was OK to travel alone from the age of eleven. But whether that meant it was OK to check in on their own, or whether the person at the check-in desk would be tricky, they didn't really know. At last it was their turn and, without daring to look at each other, they walked up and placed their tickets on the counter.

The check-in lady had purple lipstick and powdery cheeks and such black sticky eyelashes that it was quite difficult to find her eyes and look in them. Long purple nails tapped on the counter. Dylan swallowed. He was probably supposed to say something.

'We're going to Lisbon, then Salvador,' he said. The purple lips squished themselves together like a slug trying to make itself small.

The check-in lady peered at him. Then she looked behind him at Floyd. Then to the left of them, and to the right.

Purple nail varnish ran all through her and had leaked out onto her nails, where it had hardened, like a beetle's shell.

'Well?' she said, her long nails tapping faster and faster, like a cavalry on charge. 'Give me your passports and letters of consent.'

Dylan handed over all the documents. The whole departure hall went quiet and everyone stopped moving. He didn't dare to turn round, but he knew absolutely everyone in the whole airport was staring at them. She opened the passports. She flicked a glance at each boy and down at their photographs.

'When's your birthday?' she asked Dylan, suspiciously.

He told her and she grunted, defeated.

'Got any hold luggage?' she asked.

'No,' the boys said in unison.

'Hmm…,' she said and her purple nails danced away

on her keyboard. There was a silence while nothing happened, and then two bits of card slid out of a printer. The check-in lady gave a theatrical sigh that blasted the whole departure hall and brought it back to life.

'Here are your boarding cards then. Gate number 18.'

EIGHT

The boys risked a quick glance at each other as they left check-in. So far, so good, but they still had to get through security. Dylan had never tried so hard to be good and obey every rule. He answered everyone in security politely, did exactly what he was told immediately and looked at all the adults with the politest possible expression on his face. This must be what adults meant when they said someone 'had a good attitude'. He didn't think he could keep it up for longer than it took to get through security and that was only about half an hour. How anyone kept it up all term was a total mystery.

And then they were through. Dylan danced around Floyd all the way along the squeaky corridor.

'We've done it! Floyd? Look!' he brandished the two boarding passes. 'We're going! What d'you reckon TAP stands for? Three... Aeronautical Penguins? The Aerodynamic Pencil? Tube of Apples and Pears?'

'Whatever it stands for will be in Portuguese,' Floyd said, smiling. 'I'm not letting myself believe it until we're on the plane.' But Dylan knew the ice in his veins had begun to melt.

Through the huge glass window in the departure lounge, Dylan watched their plane arrive and line up with the passageway. It looked like a toy, only bigger. It was clearly much, much too heavy to fly. It would be like getting on a bus and launching it into space and hoping it didn't fall down. A squirt of hot lava shot through his guts.

'Hey, Floyd,' he said.

'What?' Floyd asked, without looking up from the printout of the map of Salvador.

'Nothing.' Floyd's obsession with seeing his brother made it hard to get through to him and Dylan still wasn't sure how much he could tell him. Dylan's stomach kept burning as if something hot was leaking into it from somewhere. His dad's cheery voice went through his head. 'You'll never get me going on one of those things, no thank you,' it said. Dylan began to wonder. Through the huge window that looked out over the runway, you could see the front of the plane: just a massive tube with great clumpy wings attached. Soon it would be 30,000 feet up in the air, and he would be inside it for hours and hours.

He swallowed. He wasn't afraid of flying. Dad was. Just because Dad was afraid didn't mean that he had to be.

At last a real voice cut off his thoughts. It was the boarding desk, telling them that Gate 18 was now open and would passengers kindly make their way with their boarding passes.

'Hello boys, travelling alone? Got your boarding passes? Well done. And your letter of permission?'

Floyd produced all of these while Dylan studied the floor tiles. The burning oil was now rolling around his stomach as if it owned the place. The main thing was not to let anyone know, especially not Floyd. So far Floyd had been alright, but Dylan wasn't completely sure about him yet. Dylan reckoned he wouldn't know until Joe was home whether or not Floyd would be a real friend, someone it was easy to be with, like Matt was.

'Good morning, boys. Welcome on board Flight 331.' The flight attendant beamed a great white insincere smile. Toothpaste. That was what ran in his veins.

'Thank you, Sir,' Dylan managed to say. This whole plane was just a great toothpaste tube of gunky air which Dylan would have to breathe for half a day and a night. Dylan made an effort to go forwards, but his feet remained the wrong side of the aeroplane doors, and he just wobbled a bit.

'Everything alright, is it?' asked the man, his flashy smile beginning to dim.

'Yup,' said Floyd, giving Dylan a poke in the back. Dylan lurched forwards: and he was in. He walked down the tiny aisle towards their seats. How had he not thought about how small the space would be? This was a million times worse than a classroom.

'D'you realise we'll be flying back in time?' Floyd said. 'It's five hours earlier in Brazil, so something strange is going to happen timewise. Like, it'll be dark at home in a couple of hours, but it won't be dark for ages in the plane cos we'll be flying back towards the sun. Isn't that weird? This is a bit like a tardis. Dylan? Don't you think?'

'Mm,' Dylan said, taking as long as he could to buckle his seatbelt. Dimly, he was aware that whatever ran in Floyd's veins was melting, but how could Floyd choose a moment like this to start being friendly? The muscles in Dylan's face felt all wrong. He could still get off. If he unbuckled himself, clambered over Floyd and the other passenger and said he didn't want to fly, they would let him off. And if the plane didn't take off very soon, he would do it, before his vision went black and his mind closed down. He gripped the armrests as the engines roared. How could he only find out *now* that he was afraid of flying? And 'afraid' didn't really cover it. It was nothing like the good scary feeling of jumping off Aberdovey pier. It was more like terror. He would never, ever be so stupid as to get on a plane again.

The aircraft began to move. It rolled forwards slowly at first, taxi-ing to the right place to take off. Then the tarmac whizzed past, and became a blur. The speed was as fast as Dylan had ever gone in a car, then faster and faster. Dylan's stomach dropped and he realised they had left the ground. Flaps on the wings swung upwards and there was a clunking sound as the wheels tucked back in to the body of the plane. The whole thing shook, wobbled, lifted a little, sank a bit and moved upwards again. He closed his eyes. He would shut down, hibernate, like a dormouse. If he wasn't actually asleep, he would pretend, even to himself, to be asleep. He pretended it so well that when they stopped in Lisbon and some lucky people got off, and a few lunatics got on, he just managed not to scramble over Floyd and make a dash for the exit.

NINE

Several hours later, Dylan woke up. He blinked, confused, then remembered where he was. Boxed in metal and plastic with no space, no fresh air, nothing natural anywhere. Blackness shone through the window. And only a few inches of plastic between him and dark nothingness for thousands of feet. A wave of panic moved through him, urging him to thrash about, but that would wake Floyd.

He would go mad if he didn't move, he knew that for certain. Maybe if he walked up and down a bit, imagined Megs was with him, he might feel more normal.

He unclicked his safety belt and, placing his feet carefully on the armrests, climbed over Floyd and the man sitting next to him. Their soft breathing didn't change. Towards the back of the plane, two members of the cabin crew were chatting and sorting trays, so he walked towards the front, patting his thigh to tell Megs to follow. Most people were asleep, their laptops folded into the pocket at the back of the seat in front. Shoes had been kicked off and jackets turned round to cover their fronts like a blanket. Everyone had red rugs pulled round their knees.

Dylan came to the curtain which separated ordinary passengers from First Class, and brushed through it. He closed his eyes and moved along, touching the edges of the seats as a guide. In his head, Megs scampered beside him, wagging and sniffing. The roaring noise was the rush of water and the wind in the trees. He was walking on grass, towards the tree that had fallen across the river where all his mates would be. He would clamber along it, over Rob and Aled's legs, past Matt, using their heads to balance, until he reached his place at the far end. He could see the grassy banks, the stones and the tumbling water, hear his friends' laughter.

His hand landed on nothing. He had reached the very front of the plane, where the toilets were, and after that, the cockpit.

Some people were awake and working. Dylan passed a woman hunched over her laptop, banging away at the keys. A man who had a notepad with Fanta printed on it and a Fanta pen still in his hand was dozing with plastic reading glasses perched on his nose. Dylan turned left again to walk down the second aisle, imaginary Megs trotting along beside him.

He closed his eyes again, tried to feel the wind on his neck and smell the damp grass. Tried to see the twilight blues between the dark leaves and the occasional sparkle on the water.

Then he tripped and fell over. When he picked himself up, he saw what had got in his way: an orange, high-heeled shoe, with a little hole at the front for one or two toes to peep out. The orange was the brightest colour in the aircraft. In fact it was the brightest colour Dylan had seen since his teacher's green highlighter pen had scrawled 'You can do better than this!' over his homework. And the shoe was very high-heeled, about as high as a pencil you've only sharpened twice.

Still on his knees, he picked the shoe up and parked it by its pair at an empty seat.

And then couldn't move.

Two things hit him in the face, both so surprising that he couldn't choose which one to think about first. On the seat was a piece of paper with the BlueBird logo emblazoned across the top and MEGS written in bold letters underneath. Dylan looked up and down the aisle. No one. The two orange high-heeled shoes stood side by side in the footwell, all alone, completely without a human being attached. He checked the sign above the toilet. Engaged, it said, in red. So he would only have to wait. He checked the piece of paper again. Maybe it was someone from BlueBird! Maybe someone important from BlueBird was in the toilet right now and Dylan could have hours to talk to her. What would she be like? A soft baby blue cardigan was draped over the headrest. A glass and two small bottles of clear liquid stood on the flip-down table. Gin, one of them said.

Then he saw that it wasn't the word MEGS, but MED5. Each capital was huge, and they all stood for a word. Manaus Eastern Docks, 5, was what it really said.

'Special Project: BlueBird Field Camp, the piece of paper said. Under the heading was a list. DELIVERY:

Digger: 1, (but it didn't say what make)

Chainsaws: 14 (same)

Cages 3m x 3m: 20, 5m x 5m: 6

The red light went off on the 'Engaged' sign. The handle turned. The door opened and a small figure came out and turned to close the door. Long golden hair hung like a curtain down the person's back, all the way down to her waist. She came towards Dylan in stockinged feet, a tiny grown-up barely taller than himself. She pulled her golden hair back and into a long ponytail as she walked. She wore sunglasses, and she seemed not to notice him as she settled into her seat, even though he was standing right by her.

'Excuse me, Miss,' he said.

Her head angled slowly up towards him. She wore what Tommo called 'hurty nose perfume'.

'Hey, kid?'

'Miss, are you... do you work for BlueBird?' Dylan cursed himself for not having any idea how to say things politely.

The lady lifted her sunglasses up onto her forehead. Green eyes, framed by thin swooping eyebrows, gazed at him.

'Huh?' she said.

Dylan thought fast. It might be best not to explain everything straight off. It might be better to find out if she was the right person to talk to.

'I saw your piece of paper with the logo on. Do you work there? I need to talk to someone there.'

'You wanna know about BlueBird?' She looked almost like a girl, but she sounded more like a cowboy. There was something strong running in her veins, something watery, but strangely powerful and with some sort of colour, purple maybe. He couldn't make sense of it.

'Er, yes.' Then he had a brainwave. The Geography competition. If he pretended it was for that until he found the right person, it might work better. 'I need to interview someone about your Special Projects to ask about the environmental impact,' he said, 'for a school competition.'

Her eyes narrowed suspiciously. 'It's all superclear on the website,' she said.

'Yes, but anyone can do that. I need more than what's on the website. I need an exclusive interview. Like, how do you choose where to do your projects? Who decides which er, farms to buy, for instance?'

Her fine eyebrows shot up. 'You sassin' me? Who put you up to this? Is your Pa on the plane?' She looked past him, down the aisle.

'No, I'm travelling with a friend. His dad works at BlueBird. His name is…'

She batted his words away with a graceful hand.

'It's a huge company, kiddo. Like, tens of thousands of people work for us. I won't know him.' She poured both small bottles into the glass and took a large gulp.

'I have to write a really good project, I have to come top of the class.' Grown-ups were suckers for a kid who wanted to learn. 'I know BlueBird is one of the top pharmaceutical companies in the world and…'

The lady interrupted him, jabbing a finger directly into Dylan's chest.

'Stop right there, kid. Let's get one thing straight. BlueBird has gotten to be THE top pharmaceutical company in the world.' There was the strength. Maybe it was gin in her veins as well as in her glass.

'Yes, yes, and I have to write the best project in the school, otherwise…'

The lady put her glass down and held out her hand.

'The best?' she asked, looking more closely at him. She held out her hand and took his in an iron handshake. 'I like ambition in a kid. You are dead right, boy. Be the best. Nothing else is worth a dime. Miss Crassy,' she drawled in a gravelly voice. 'Special Projects Manager of BlueBird. I have to be supercareful who I speak to.' She shook her golden mane sadly. 'There are some mean old journalists out there who would do anything to get an interview. Trip me up and twist my words.' She tilted her head on one side, looking him up and down. 'You have a passion for this project of yours. I like that. How old are you, hon?'

'Eleven.'

'Hmm. Pity,' she said, almost to herself. 'So. BlueBird is the best company in the world. We've got that straight. No more of this 'one of the top five' baloney. Ask away.'

'How I can meet the CEO?'

She leant back in her seat and laughed. 'Speak to the CEO? You gotta be kidding me. For starters you'd need to be at least twenty years older. Then you'd need to be either a President or Head of the United Nations or summat. Then you'd need to come up with a mighty brilliant new idea for the product of the future. Believe me it is darned tricksy to get the attention of the CEO, and I've been trying for –'

At that moment a member of the cabin crew came up behind Dylan.

'Excuse me, young man, passengers have paid a great deal for the privacy and quiet of first class and I'm afraid I have to ask you to leave.'

'But…' Dylan looked desperately at Miss Crassy. He had only just started. She smiled at him and fished out a card from her briefcase.

'Take this,' she said. 'It's got the number for my office in Salvador. You can speak to Anton, my secretary. He's superhelpful. I'll tell him to give you all the info you need.'

'Will you be there?' Dylan asked.

She gave a huge smile and held out her thumb and forefinger close together to show something very small.

'For two tiny minutes.' She took a long gulp of her drink and her eyes glazed over. 'Then I'm going north to Manaus, and up the Amazon to our field camp. After which,' she looked at her glass and seemed to be talking to herself, 'Thursday.' She shook her head slowly and dropped her voice to a whisper, 'Boy, will I give him something to listen to then!'

Dylan had no idea what she was talking about.

'Thursday?' he asked.

Her eyes snapped wide open and fixed on him.

'You still here? Scram, kid. Time's up. I need my beauty sleep.'

Dylan got back to his seat and looked out of the window. He had got a lead. Before they had even landed! This time, he thought of the whole world of water below him, glistening and glinting in the starlight. All that life in the sea, swimming, darting, diving, floating, wafting and creeping in the depths and along the sandy bottom. He was in the same world as the sea and all that life. There was just a bit of gap between them. Quite a big gap. The boiling feeling began in his stomach again.

He woke Floyd up with a shove to the shoulder.

'Hey, Floyd, wake up. I've just met a lady from BlueBird. She gave me her card. I'm going to get an interview.'

Floyd rubbed his eyes.

'Huh. Great. With the CEO?'

'Er, well, she said her assistant would help me find the right person to speak to.'

Floyd leaned over him to look out of the window to where the blackness was giving way to midnight blue on the horizon. 'Hey, look, it's so amazing. You can see land.'

Dylan thought that seeing land dozens of miles below you was not a good thing. A good thing was when you could see land right there between your feet.

A gentle ding-dong sounded and the picture of the seat belt lit up above Dylan's head. The cabin crew's voice came over the sound system.

'Please tighten your seatbelts as we are now beginning the descent into Salvador.'

Salvador lay beneath them in darkness except for a golden dewy spider's web of lights showing the motorways, main roads and, as they grew closer, smaller streets. In the centre, the spider's web showed a tidy grid, but on the edges of the city the lines became closer together, more wiggly and fainter. The houses and roads must be packed together in those parts. Dylan remembered his conversation with Tommo and wondered if two boys were sleeping in bunk beds in the same room somewhere down there.

As they came closer, and dawn began to break, he could see that the hills were covered with tiny houses, all crammed in together so tightly you couldn't see the roads between them. The houses swarmed up the hillsides and down into the valleys, but in the centre of the city there were skyscrapers, motorways, block after block of high-rise buildings. The plane flew on and on over the enormous city. For the first time Dylan wondered if it would be possible to find Joe and Mac in such a huge place.

A great clunk sounded as the aircraft's wheels came down from the undercarriage. It was lighter now: Dylan could see individual houses and washing hung out on the balconies of blocks of flats. People shot past as the plane came closer and closer to the ground. Cars flashed by. The wheels thumped the ground. A blur of green could be seen outside the window; as Dylan watched, it became less blurry, until the plane came to a halt and the separate blades of thick, spiny grass could be seen in the early morning light.

'It's greener than at home,' said Floyd. 'Everyone says the grass in Wales is so green, but this is even greener.'

'It's darker,' said Dylan, loyally. 'Not greener.'

TEN

'OK. We need tickets for the Salvador metro,' Floyd said, his voice rich and full of confidence.

At the ticket office, Dylan pointed to himself and Floyd and the name of the station they needed to go to on the map. The man nodded and printed out two tickets and slid them under the glass.

There was only one line, so it was easy. Before long they stood on a platform, got on a train, waited for two stops and got off at the third. At the correct exit they looked at each other and burst out laughing.

'You look so surprised!' Floyd said.

'So do you!'

'Joe lives about four streets away,' said Floyd. 'It's Tuesday, isn't it? And it's nearly breakfast time. He might be about to leave for school.' He took a folded piece of paper out of his pocket and opened it up to show a street map. 'They live at 345 Avenida Emidio Navarro. Look, we're here. We have to go…' Floyd turned the paper round, '…this way.'

At number 345, Floyd rang the bell. They could hear someone shuffling towards the door. A thin man in black with sad eyes opened the door, looking over their heads, then down at them.

Floyd gave his dad's name, and his brother's. 'My family,' he said.

'Sua familia?'

The man shook his head very slowly, shrugged and rubbed his long nose. He seemed to have something like tea running in his veins. Just ordinary, weak tea. His voice was deep and started off slow, but it picked up speed as he went along. He started throwing his arms about, and miming strange movements. His voice grew louder and more desperate.

'What on earth's he saying?' asked Floyd.

But from the man's tone and arm movements it was very clear to Dylan.

'I think he means they're not here. He might mean,' Dylan hesitated, 'that they have been taken away.'

Floyd turned to the man. 'Joe's not here?' he said, in a voice agonised enough to be understood in any language.

The man shook his head as slowly as it was possible to shake a head. It was so slow that Dylan thought he was hoping something would happen to make him change his mind in mid-shake.

'Joe foi embora,' he said, and to show them what he meant, put two long arms around Floyd and dragged him a few steps away.

'Hey!' yelled Floyd.

The man nodded.

'There was some sort of fight?' Dylan asked, miming with his fists.

The man's sad eyes looked even sadder.

Floyd turned his back on the man and stared at the lamp post. His body congealed into a tight frozen unit, and Dylan saw the blue fade and fade until only clear ice crept through his friend's veins. The man opened the door a little wider and said something.

'Hey, Floyd. He's saying we can go in. We haven't got anywhere else to go. We need to think about what to do.'

'They're not here?' Floyd's voice was so low, Dylan could hardly hear it. 'We've come five thousand, five hundred and sixty-eight miles and they're not here?'

'Floyd, come on, let's get inside.' Dylan edged Floyd through the door and up a flight of stairs. Floyd moved like a zombie, arms limp, expressionless.

The door to Mac and Joe's apartment was difficult to open and once they had managed it, they saw why. What must have been a tower of lever arch files had fallen in front of the door, creating a barrier. Once they had stepped over the heaps and reached the living room, Dylan wasn't so sure there had ever been a tidy pile.

You couldn't see the walls. Newspaper articles, photos and what looked like maps of rivers overlapped each other. Photos of animals, ripped out of magazines, were tacked to the wall. Their names were inked in black beneath the photos, each one with a question mark after it. Honey bears? one read, under the picture of something that looked more like a monkey. Capybaras? another said, under what looked like a monster guinea pig. Amazonian Field Camp, BlueBird, said one piece of paper with 'IT'S BLOODY MURDER' scrawled underneath it.

Dylan moved swiftly on, thinking that Mac might be madder than Floyd had realised, and came to a calendar with a day circled several times in red pen. It had 'MUST BE STOPPED. BUT HOW?' scrawled next to it. The date was Thursday 24 October, just two days from now.

'Wow,' Dylan said.

There was nowhere to sit. The room was full of small hills and valleys of magazines, papers, books and ring-bound files. There might have been a sofa and a coffee table underneath, but you couldn't be sure. Some of the books and magazines lay half-open, others had post-it notes sticking out of them. It seemed to have snowed scrunched-up balls of paper: dozens of them lay everywhere, flung into every corner. Dylan picked one up and smoothed it out. The printed page had hand-written scrawls all over it, pointing to parts of the text. 'National Geographic' was printed across the top.

'Dear Sir,' it read. 'Thank you for your letter. If what you say is true, it would be a scandal of the highest order. Please contact us again if you are ever able to produce evidence supporting your suspicions.'

'It's been burgled. Someone must have been looking for something, whoever took them away.'

'No,' Floyd said, dully. 'This is normal for my dad.'

'He beats Gramp, then,' Dylan said.

Dylan opened files at random and flicked through them. One was about parrots, one about monkeys and another about something that he had never heard of and couldn't tell whether it was the size of a single bacterium or a diplodocus. Then he found one all about bats: vampire bats, greater bulldog bats and moustache bats. Back home, they had mainly pipistrelles and brown long-eared bats, which swooped around the barn and along the river. Every time they came out, and their odd black forms shot past him, always at an angle, Dylan felt their speed race through him and tried to follow their mad darting flights with his eyes. And here, in what looked like a boring file, was loads of stuff about them. It was funny to think you could have a job which let you read about bats.

'If they're not here, they could be anywhere,' Floyd said. 'They might have left Brazil.' He gave a harsh laugh. 'We might as well go straight back to the airport. We'll never find them now.' Floyd picked his way over the piles of papers out of the living room and back towards the front door. When he reached it, he slumped down against it, banging the letterbox.

Dylan unscrunched several more snowballs, and found that all the letters said pretty much the same thing. He would have to think fast. This might be a disaster. He, Dylan, would still be able to go to BlueBird and find someone to talk to but, if they had to go back without even seeing Joe, Floyd would freeze to the point of splintering into pieces. There must be something in all this mess that could help him work out where they were.

Dylan wandered through the flat, stepping over, between and sometimes even on, papers and books. He came to a bedroom with a double bed. There was only just enough room to sleep. Most of the bed was the same as the rest of the flat: heaped with papers and magazines. *World Wildlife Organisation*, said one. *Conservation Magazine, Permaculture, Ecomagazine.* They all seemed to be about woods or lakes or rivers or farms or mountains. Dylan had had no idea there were whole magazines about land. Dad had the Screwfix catalogue, which was about, well, tools and screws and fixing things, and Mum had a magazine called *Grow It*, and neither of those seemed interesting. But these, well, Dylan could see that on a rainy day you just might want to have a look at one of these.

On his way back down the corridor, Dylan pushed open another door and stood at the entrance of an extraordinary room.

The single bed was made and the edge of the bedspread, patterned with racing cars, hung horizontally over the carpet. Three small cars were parked centrally on the window sill, all facing forwards and at the same distance from each other. Many more cars, in lines as if they were in an airport car park, were grouped at one end. A pair of slippers, tidily next to each other, peeped out from under the bed. A book on the bedside table lined up precisely with the table's corner. A pencil holder, full of coloured pencils, every single one of which was sharpened to a fine point, marked the centre of the table.

Dylan stepped into the room. He opened the cupboard door. Inside, small jumpers, neatly folded all the same way, lay in one pile on the shelf. Below this was a rail from which hung three mini white shirts, a blazer and a pair of trousers. It was as tidy as a shop. A timetable on the cupboard door listed lessons and chores to do after school. 'Remind Dad to buy food', it said on Monday, 'Remind Dad to wash clothes', on Tuesday, 'Remind Dad to pay electricity', on Wednesday.

Joe's room. Mac couldn't have kept it this tidy. *So Joe must have.* There was an aura of calm in the room that made Dylan want to stay. In there, he could forget the chaos of the rest of the flat. And the mess they had got themselves into.

A clatter came from behind him, then Floyd's voice cried out. Dylan rushed back, tripping over papers and mess, to where Floyd was still sitting on the floor by the front door, clutching handfuls of envelopes. The letterbox had fallen off the door and post was spilling out of it.

'Hey, look at this!' he said, his eyes full of hope.

'What is it?' asked Dylan.

'Dad's post!'

'So?'

'It's all unopened! Here are letters from my mum, some from me to Joe. Here's the one from the Courts of Justice. He hasn't read any of them. They were all stuffed into the letterbox. He's never emptied it!'

'What's so great about that?'

'It means he doesn't know about the court action to make him bring Joe home, of course.'

'So he wasn't being horrible,' Dylan said. 'He's just...' the word 'mad' hovered on his lips, but Floyd might never forgive him if he said that.

'Mad!' said Floyd. 'He's always been mad. Mad is what we're used to. His whole idea of going to Brazil was mad. We just weren't used to him being unreasonable.'

Dylan shook his head. 'You can be mad but reasonable?'

'I mean sort of unkind, you know. He's always been kind. When he remembered to think about anything apart from work, that is. So it was odd that he wasn't even answering his post.'

Seeing Floyd come back to life shifted something in Dylan's brain. There had been something unsettling about Miss Crassy, but at least she spoke English. Perhaps she could help them.

'Floyd, we can ring the lady I met on the plane. We can ring Miss Crassy.'

'Who?'

'The one who works at BlueBird. She'll help us.'

'It's a multi-national company, Dylan. It employs eighty thousand people. I don't think she'll know anything about Dad.'

'Yes, but they need to know if something has happened to one of their employees, don't they? I've got her card, we can ring her right now.'

Floyd nodded and pulled out his phone. Once he had dialled, he put the phone on speaker.

'Ola?' A male voice through the phone.

'Could I speak to Miss Crassy, please?'

'This is her secretary. You can talk to me.'

'Oh. We're looking for Mr Adams, Sir. Do you know him? Only he works for the same company as you. We came all the way from Wales to see him but we think something bad has happened. He's not at home and … we don't know what to do.'

Silence.

'Who is speaking?'

'I'm Mr Adams's son.'

'Joe?'

'No, I'm his brother, Floyd. We've come a long way, but we think … something's wrong. He's disappeared.'

Another long silence.

'No. I don't know a Mr Adams. I can't help you.

Goodbye.' The phone went dead. Floyd slid off the stack of papers he was sitting on and landed on the floor.

'Hang on,' said Dylan. 'One minute he knows your brother's called Joe and the next minute he's never heard of your dad. That doesn't make sense.'

The phone's shrill tone rang out and Floyd pressed answer.

'Hello?'

'Is this Mr Adams's son?' A woman's voice spoke.

'It's Miss Crassy!' hissed Dylan.

'Yes, do you know my dad?' answered Floyd, frowning at Dylan to keep quiet.

'Sure I do. I have to apologise for my colleague, he gets himself all muddled up. I do know where Mr Adams is. You are his son, are you? What did you say your name was?'

'Floyd. You know where my father is?'

'Yes, and I'd be real happy to help you reach your father.' Even over the phone Dylan could sense the strange strength in her voice. 'I should warn you though – he's not well. Perhaps you would like to come with me? I can provide transport.'

'Really? That's ... thank you! Thank you!'

'Where are you now?'

'At Dad's flat.' Floyd gave the address.

'I'll be there in thirty mins. Be ready to leave.' And there was that bite, the sharpness again. Perhaps because she was such a busy, important woman. The phone went dead.

ELEVEN

'I can't believe it,' said Floyd. 'She's going to take us to him. It might all be OK after all.'

'And she knows the CEO, too. I'm hungry.' As Dylan walked over to the fridge he had a sudden vision of fat slices of pink ham and wedges of cheese and pickle and four-packs of chocolate mousse and maybe some jelly that Joe hadn't finished. He opened the door and his heart sank. 'Three old-fashioned camera films. One bottle of lemonade, empty. Four blackened, bent and shrivelled carrots. A plastic container of what might have been hummus, but which has been scraped out. Something oval, grey and furry.'

'That used to drive Mum crazy,' said Floyd, sadly. 'Even if he'd finished something, he'd put the container back in the fridge.'

'When you say "mad"…' Dylan hesitated.

'Not dangerous mad,' said Floyd. 'Just always thinking about his work. Always. Sometimes we'd be having tea and he would get up in the middle of telling us a story and go into his study and write something down. It might take an hour. Then he'd come back – we would have cleared up and be watching TV and he would carry on telling us the story without a word missing, as if the conversation was still happening.'

'Is he very clever?'

'He says he isn't. He says he just works harder than most people, but I sometimes wonder.'

'He does sound quite annoying.'

'Oh, yes, he's very annoying,' Floyd said, but his face softened.

At that moment a deep rumble came from outside. It grew louder and louder, then it softened. Dylan clambered over piles to the window.

'Holy Moses. She's come in a stretch limo!'

Floyd came up beside him. A sleek dark limousine purred by the pavement. The driver got out and opened one of the passenger doors.

'She's got a chauffeur! With a hat!'

One of the orange shoes, followed by a neatly trousered leg emerged from the open door. Miss Crassy straightened up and stood, fiddling with her cuffs, on the pavement. She gazed first up, then down the street. She nodded at her chauffeur and strode to the door.

The doorbell rang out: one short, sharp ring. They both jolted at the sound as if a burst of electricity had shot through them.

Floyd gathered up his rucksack, put his coat on and pressed the buzzer to open the door.

It swung open but all that came in was a shadow, cast by the hallway light. The shadow moved further into the room, and again, her shiny orange shoes appeared before Miss Crassy did. She stood in the doorway, ignoring them, but gazing around, just as she had done in the street.

'So this is how he lives,' she said. Without even glancing at either of them, she came in, and, stepping over piles of magazines, walked the length of the sitting-room wall. 'Hmmm,' she said.

'Where are my dad and brother, Miss?' asked Floyd.

Miss Crassy glanced at Floyd and immediately lost interest in the rest of the room. She gazed at Floyd for a long moment.

'Good Lord,' she said. 'So you are Mac's other son.' She walked around him, picking her way over papers and files, looking at him from every angle, nodding.

'Miss Crassy, what do you mean, my dad isn't well? What's the matter with him?'

Miss Crassy pulled her sunglasses off and looked at Floyd with sorrowful eyes. 'It's an illness many people get and it's temporary. It's a form of malaria. He has delusions, imaginary enemies. It's, like, so sad,' she said, kindly. 'He started attacking BlueBird. We've given him a holiday from work, at the field camp. We're looking after Joe there, too. The alternative was to fire him, but that would have increased his paranoia and fed his theories. All he needs is rest away from the stresses of work and the world and he will recover. We're superproud of the way we look after our staff.'

'Has he seen a doctor?' Dylan asked, picking up his rucksack.

Miss Crassy swung round and noticed Dylan for the first time.

'You!' she said. 'Why didn't you tell me your friend was Mr Adams's son? He's seen a ton of doctors. We have in-house doctors caring for all our staff. You needn't worry, little Mister.' She turned back to Floyd. 'They're in Manaus. Or near there, anyway. It's a plane ride away. Get your things. Let's go. We haven't much time.'

Another plane. Dylan dropped his rucksack.

'You can leave me here. I've got to go to the BlueBird office. It's OK,' he said, as Miss Crassy frowned. 'I'll go on my own. I know the way, I can walk. Then I'll come back here and wait for you and Joe, Floyd.'

Miss Crassy's frown deepened. 'That's not going to work.' She turned to face Dylan straight on. She appeared to be thinking.

'Tell you what,' she said. 'You can ask me stuff about BlueBird in the plane. OK?'

'Um, the school project is all about talking to, er, several people. I really need to go to the office.'

Miss Crassy made an irritated noise and looked at her watch.

'Looksee, I have absolutely zip-diddly time to waste. My plane leaves in under an hour.' Then she smacked the palm of her hand against her forehead. 'Hey, what am I thinking? There's no one in the office anyway. The CEO and everyone are in Manaus this week, at the BlueBird Annual Conference.' She threw her hands into the air. 'Win-win, guys! Everybody happy. Come on then, both of you, vamos!'

Dylan followed Floyd through the door and into the limo with a dragging feeling in his gut. She hadn't mentioned the BlueBird conference on the plane when he said he wanted to meet the CEO, so how come she just remembered it now? Did she just make it up to get him to come? But if it was true, and if the CEO was there… He followed Floyd with one leg happy to go forward and the other wanting to turn round. Up until now, he had felt in control of what they were doing, and looking forward to telling Matt and everyone about it. It was good to have Miss Crassy's help, wasn't it? So why did he feel weird about it? Why was he not so sure he would want to tell them this bit?

The limo was so long you could hardly see the face of a man in a grey suit who sat in a far corner. It had a faint flowery smell that made you think of money and the seat practically hugged Dylan when he sat in it.

The chauffeur closed the door silently behind them and slid into the driver's seat. The purring, which had never stopped, grew to a roar again and the great car oozed away down the road and curled around the corner.

TWELVE

The limo drove back across the strange, hot city, where smart skyscrapers stood right next to damaged buildings with crumbling walls and no windows. Everything looked dusty, as if it hadn't rained for months. At one point they stopped at some traffic lights.

'Oh,' said Dylan.

'What?' Floyd asked as they moved off again.

'The lights. They go red, orange, green, just like at home. I thought they'd go brown, pink, yellow or something.' As he said this, the sky went black. Dylan blinked and realised the limo had entered a long dark tunnel. His eyes adjusted, and he saw the tunnel was formed by hundreds and hundreds of giant bamboos, with huge trunks as thick as any tree's. The bamboo forest towered over the car and nearly met overhead. It was like suddenly becoming an ant in a field of long grass. Birmingham airport had been surprisingly different from home, but this was beginning to feel like a different planet.

It turned out that when Miss Crassy had said 'my plane', she meant exactly that. They cruised right onto the runway and up to a small plane with only eight windows and came to a stop so gently that Dylan couldn't pinpoint the moment when the car actually stopped moving.

'Blimey,' Floyd whispered. 'She's got a private plane.'

'Would you, Anton?' asked Miss Crassy, and the man in the grey suit emerged from the seat at the far end. He tidied his tie and did up the buttons on his jacket in slow smooth movements, glancing at the boys as he did so. And in that one glance Dylan got a clear sense of cream: rich, milky-white cream that looked perfect to pour on apple pie or porridge, or to whip up and plonk on jammy scones. What he couldn't immediately make sense of was a nasty tang in the cream. But then he got it. It had gone off. It looked delicious, but it would be sharp and sour. Rank. One taste on your lips would make you retch.

The man got out of the car and approached the plane. He pulled a panel in the side of the plane downwards to form three steps. Then he pulled the lowest step which opened out again to form one more at just the right height from the ground.

'Another plane,' Dylan said, his insides heaving. How had he gone so quickly from being in control to not really having any choice? Now he was stuck at the airport without any way of finding the BlueBird offices, or even how to get back to Mac's flat.

'We're late,' Miss Crassy said. 'Just grab your things and get in, can you?'

Inside, the plane was almost exactly the same as the limo. Everything was nearly a colour. The pale leather seats were not quite caramel. The carpet was nearly white. The window frames looked as if they were trying to be grey but hadn't quite made it. Somehow it wasn't as bad as being in the first plane. The burning feeling came but it went again. The ceiling seemed higher and there was more space between the seats. It felt more like being in a space-age living room than being in an aircraft.

'Everything is the colour of a week-old calf,' Dylan said. 'All creamy and clean.' He tried to imagine Gramp sitting here, in this plane, in his old pyjama bottoms and holey jumper and decided Gramp had probably never been anywhere so clean in his entire life. Then he thought of Tommo. Here he was, dreading another a flight, when Tommo would have been jumping up and down with excitement. There was something scary about being able to imagine what his family were doing when he knew that they had no idea where he was. He sat down, cautiously, waiting for his stomach to roll, but it didn't happen. As soon as they had buckled their safety belts, the plane took off. There was no waiting, no fuss about safety equipment. They were airborne in moments.

Dylan and Floyd sat opposite each other, both with window seats. Miss Crassy sat across the aisle at a small table. Dylan swallowed and put on his most polite, grown-up voice.

'Miss Crassy, can I ask you more questions now?' he asked. 'I didn't get a chance to finish on the plane to Salvador.'

Miss Crassy frowned, then seemed to remember.

'Oh yes. Environmental policies, isn't it? We are supercool on those.'

'Yes, but can you tell me exactly what you do? Can I see something working in the field camp?'

'In the field camp? How do you know about the...' Miss Crassy looked shocked, then recovered herself. 'Certainly. You can see a whole load of stuff when we're there. We'll land in Manaus and take a car and then a boat from there. In fact,' she looked at each of them in turn, 'I think we'll take two cars. I'll go ahead with Floyd – you know, to give him a chance to see his dad again in private...'

'And brother,' Floyd said.

'Yes. Of course. You, boy, will follow on in another car.' She turned to Anton, slouched in grey in the far corner. 'Hey, Anton, ring for a second car, will you? You can take care of eco-kid here, yeah? You could show him around, show him the sights of Manaus, perhaps. Just make sure you take care of him.' The man raised one eyebrow and gave a nod.

'And there'll be plenty of chances to talk later, young man. Now, excuzee me, but I need to catch up with some correspondence.' She took out a slim laptop and some earphones and plugged herself in.

Dylan and Floyd glanced at each other and at Miss Crassy, who was bent over the keyboard, tapping away furiously.

'As soon as I've seen Joe I'll ask them to bring you along, OK?' Floyd whispered.

'Sure,' Dylan whispered back, trying to sound as if a morning's sightseeing with Anton wasn't sending alarm bells clanging through his chest.

'Hey, look, is that the rainforest?' Floyd said, after a while, his head against the window.

Below them was nothing but dark green: a huge, spreading fluffy carpet. No matter what angle Dylan looked through the window, to the left or right, far ahead or behind, there was nothing but green fur beneath them, thick, dense, dark, bottle-green. Dylan didn't know how high up they were, or anything to do with maths and distance, but it was obvious that he was looking over miles and miles and miles of rainforest. Or more specifically – and his heart lurched when he understood – at thousands and thousands no, millions and millions of trees. His mind spun as he imagined himself down there, lost among the trees, surrounded by acres and acres of nothing but trees and wild animals.

Dylan couldn't take his eyes off it. In Wales there were

plenty of wild places, where hill after hill rolled on and on and lay down in the distance and changed from green to dusty blue as they got further away, but they weren't covered, as this place was, with trees. In Wales, the trees had all been cleared to make grazing land for sheep, or cut down to build boats. They were bald hills, most of them, covered only with heather and gorse and – in the summer – sweet black bilberries. He pressed his head against the window again. Matt would never believe there could be so many trees and Dylan wasn't sure he would be able to describe the hugeness of it. He wondered what Matt was doing now, on the trip to Harlech. They were six hours behind in Salvador and it was nearly lunchtime here so it would be… about six in the evening there. Matt would have had his first day, collecting mud and river water and stones and different plants and now they would all be eating in the canteen. Rob would be saying something no one could understand and Aled would answer with something gloomy.

On they flew, on and on, and still the carpet of green remained unchanged. He couldn't explain to himself exactly why, but he would have done anything to be down there, right in the middle of the rainforest.

Then he was blinded by a golden flash. Dylan blinked. A trail of glittering water split the forest like a wedge, and Dylan realised he was looking at the Amazon river itself. Strangely, it was two-tone, split down its length: one half was black, the other sandy. It was as if one half were made of molasses, the thick brown sweet treacle Mum made gingerbread with, and the other half of fudge. Dylan's nose didn't leave the window until the rainforest grew thinner and the plane lost height and the city of Manaus came into view.

At the airport, two cars were indeed waiting for them, right on the tarmac where the plane came to a halt. Miss Crassy tottered down the steps of the plane in her orange high-heeled shoes, with one hand around Floyd's wrist. Floyd turned to look at Dylan just before he slid into the car, and all Dylan could see on his face was confusion. Dylan felt it too: why would she be holding on to him like that when he was so keen to go anyway? Dylan waved, putting off the moment when he had to look up at Anton and get into a car with him. Eventually Floyd's car was out of sight and Dylan obeyed Anton's silent gesture. He got into the back seat in slow motion, trying to work out if he had a choice. The trouble was, he was feeling less and less sure he believed Miss Crassy when she said the CEO was in Manaus. A great fat slug of uncertainty moved in his stomach. Mum would have a fit if she knew where he was. He had a nasty feeling that even Dad would be worried.

He swallowed. He was being stupid. Floyd's dad worked for BlueBird and so did Anton. It was a huge, multinational company. Anton might be a nasty guy to be in business with – Dylan was sure of that – but he wore a suit and tie.

He wasn't going to do anything to Dylan. So Dylan couldn't understand why he suddenly longed to be in the kitchen at home with Tommo, eating toast and Mum's homemade strawberry jam, stroking Megs or going round asking everyone in the village for hammers so they could all work on the treehouse at the same time. And then he remembered: if he didn't succeed here, they would never build a treehouse. It was exactly because it was so great being at home that he was here. He pulled himself together. Just because a plan changed a bit when you were actually doing it didn't mean the plan wasn't a good one.

THIRTEEN

They reached a three-lane motorway clogged with
stationary traffic. Winding between the cars, people
with baskets on their heads tried to sell bananas, crisps,
bottles of water, candyfloss in pink, blue or green,
melons, nuts, strawberries. It was like Machynlleth
market gone mad, with everyone right in the middle of
the road until the lights changed and they had to shoot
back to the pavement. A yellow motorbike with TAXI
written on the fuel tank passed Dylan's window, and he
was astonished to see a mum carrying a baby, a dad and
a little girl, all squashed up behind the driver. Along the
road, brightly coloured graffiti covered the walls: huge
fat lettering turned into faces that were winking or
laughing. They came to a man holding small wooden
cages and as the car slowed at a junction Dylan glimpsed

colourful butterflies in the cages, flapping against the wooden bars.

At the next set of traffic lights a large plastic sign made Dylan's heart leap: Amazonia Conferencia BlueBird, it said, with an arrow pointing to the left. Dylan sat bolt upright. Even he could understand that meant BlueBird's Amazon Conference. Portuguese was so easy. So Miss Crassy hadn't lied! And in three languages underneath it read 'Manaus Opera House'. The slug shrivelled away to nothing.

'I have to get out!' he said, rattling the handle. 'Anton, the door's locked. Can you tell the driver to stop?' The CEO would be right there, just a few hundred metres away. Dylan only needed about half an hour, then they could be on their way again.

The lights changed to green.

'Anton?'

Anton shook his head and Dylan had to watch the sign growing smaller in the distance. He told himself that maybe Anton was right, it was better to regroup with Miss Crassy and Floyd before going to the Conference, but it was still agony, having been so close.

Views of the river flashed between buildings but it seemed to be getting further away.

'Aren't we meeting them at the docks? Where the boat is?' he asked, but Anton ignored him.

They passed right through the city until they came to a petrol station with a road leading up a hill beside it. It was a narrow road with only room for one car and on either side were shops, tiny shops, just two arms' span wide. A bike shop – more like a beach stall with a corrugated roof – didn't sell whole new bikes, it sold bits of bikes: an assortment of wheels, handlebars, frames, and chains. Next to it was a pet shop with a blue and black canary in a cage. Dylan just caught its button black eye before the car moved on. The houses were jumbled up together, some of them just brick shelters with corrugated iron roofs and patched-up walls. Some had been built on top of others and not finished. Bare brick openings for windows didn't always have glass in them. Dylan realised that it was a poor area, poorer than anywhere in Wales. But the people, just like Gramp said, looked the same as they did in Machynlleth High Street: busy, chatting, going somewhere, discussing business. They passed a brightly coloured school playground with yelling children, and a library whose doors were open to the street. Dylan thought it must be nice to live in a country where it was so hot you didn't ever have to close the doors.

The trouble was, it didn't seem a the part of town Miss Crassy would go to. And it seemed to be getting poorer. The tarmac gave out and they drove along a dirt track with a gutter of running water down one side. All the houses now were just rough shelters, mostly wooden, with tin or plastic roofs. Some were on stilts, with piles of rubbish scattered around their legs. A rat darted from one heap of torn plastic bags to another.

A young man sat crosslegged in a doorway, with something long and metallic on his lap.

'Was that a gun?' Dylan asked, as the car moved on, but Anton turned his head away.

The car had to crawl along now that the dirt track was so narrow. Electric cables in chaotic tangles stretched across the road from the shacks on one side to the other. A group of children, barefoot, ran along the side of the car, calling and holding out their hands. The car picked up speed to pass them and took a turning to the left, then the right, then the right again, until Dylan was no longer sure which direction they had come from. When the track became impossible, the driver turned the car around and came to a stop. As Anton leant over Dylan to unlock the door, the tang of sour cream spiked in Dylan's brain.

'Out,' Anton said. 'With your luggage.'

'Where...?' asked Dylan, grabbing his rucksack and gazing around at the rickety houses. 'Are we meeting Floyd here?'

Anton gave a short laugh, more like a bark, and jerked his chin up to underline his meaning. Dylan climbed out, pulling his rucksack behind him and turned to see Anton glaring at him as he reached over and slammed the door. The car pulled away and drove off, leaving Dylan staring at the back of Anton's head through the rear windscreen.

FOURTEEN

Dylan's guts shrivelled. The air was hot and thick after the cool car, so thick, that in his paralysed shock he felt it might be the only thing holding him up.

As flies swarmed around him, the smell shifted from something nearly pleasant, like very ripe melon, to something that would make you back out of a toilet, fast. The seconds ticked by and the truth filtered down into his brain. Anton had dumped him. He hadn't 'taken care' of him at all. Miss Crassy would be furious. Unless … Dylan's brain melted a little in the sweaty heat. In gangster films 'take care of' meant something completely different.

Dampness around his toes told him he was standing in smelly water. He leapt out of the drain, brown sludge sticking to the sides of his trainers. He shook the flies off and ran after the car, dodging the rubbish and the drains.

The car had turned left, but when he took the same corner, it wasn't there. Narrow tracks led off between the shacks, some too narrow for a car, but some wide enough. Dylan ran a short way up one of these, his mind racing, thoughts popping about in his head.

The idea that he had to get back to the Manaus Opera House and the conference as quickly as possible was overtaken by an uneasy feeling that speaking to the CEO might not be his biggest problem.

The track narrowed. He ran back and chose another one. The same. He took a side alley, not caring where he trod anymore, darting this way and that, adrenaline giving him wings. This couldn't be happening. He didn't speak Portuguese, he had no money, no phone. After a while, breathless and unable to think of what to do next, he stopped at yet another rough crossroads between collapsing homes and muddy pathways. Nobody knew where he was. Even Anton probably couldn't find him now.

With an ache in his gut he let something sink into his mind. It was a truth he could hardly bear to know. Anton had not disobeyed Miss Crassy. She had meant to get rid of him. And if she could do that, order Anton to lose him in Manaus (surely the poorest part of the poorest area was his own genius idea), then it meant no one would come to find him. In fact it meant many things, and each one of them hit him over the head like so many bricks. If Miss Crassy had ordered Anton to lose him in Manaus, it meant she had never had any intention of taking Dylan back to Salvador. It meant she couldn't ever let Floyd go back to Salvador and home either, because he would ask where Dylan was. It meant she couldn't take Floyd to Mac and Joe, because Floyd would tell them Anton had lost Dylan in Manaus, and Mac, a grown-up, would try to do something about it when he was better.

Unless.

Unless she never intended to let Mac, Joe or Floyd ever leave the field camp.

Aled's words came back to him 'murdered in Brazil and never heard of again'. Dylan swung round, sure someone was watching him, but no one was there. A burst of laughter made him look up. Across the way from where he stood, a group of teenagers were sitting on a balcony, slumped against a bare breeze-block wall, drinking beer from bottles and laughing. One of them was swaying on his feet, eyes half closed, holding his bottle so loosely that beer spilled out of it. One of the others pushed him, and they all joined in, shoving and pushing him, pulling his hair and laughing. He dropped the bottle, which rolled around, pouring beer off the edge of the balcony. His eyes closed and he collapsed in a heap, one arm dangling down between the railings. The others howled with laughter for a while, then settled themselves down with their bottles, looking bored now and disappointed.

Under the balcony hung dozens of the small wooden

cages Dylan had seen earlier when they were driving through the city centre. In each one flashed a colour: purple, orange, yellow. Butterflies. Each one of them probably desperate for nectar.

As Dylan's breathing slowed, his thoughts began to make sense. He had to get back to the centre of Manaus. He had to talk to the CEO, and get help to find Floyd.

Dylan swivelled round again. No one. Someone was watching him, he was sure of it. But there was laughter and when he turned back again, the kids were on him, surrounding him, calling, laughing, pulling at his clothes. At first he thought they wanted to play. He managed a smile and caught their hands. But then they were pulling, yanking, everything: his trousers down, his T-shirt up, his rucksack. He pulled his trousers up and his rucksack slid off his shoulder. A cry went up and the pack of kids ran off, tossing his rucksack between them, screaming and yelling. He ran after them, calling out, but they were too fast for him and when he turned a corner after them, they had disappeared.

Now he had lost his ticket home and his passport. Now he could die here and no one would even know who he was. Had been. Where he came from.

If he wasn't so scared, he would have been really, really angry. And if he wasn't so angry, he would have been scared out of his wits. How could he have been so stupid? Why did he get in Anton's car when he knew he didn't trust him? He knew his creaminess was sour and wrong.

Why had he even got in Miss Crassy's car? Even she had had that nasty tang, and if he hadn't been so bull-headed, as Gramp would put it, about getting his farm back, he would never have got in her car. In fact, what on earth had he been thinking, flying all the way to Brazil with Floyd? Suddenly he didn't care about anything except getting out of this place and back to somewhere where teenagers didn't have guns, and kids weren't in thieving gangs.

Only a few minutes ago, he thought things had got as bad as they could get and yet now he had lost his rucksack with everything in it. If this was snakes and ladders he had slid right off the bottom of the board. How much worse could things get?

As if in answer, a great crack and rumble came from the sky. Fat drops bounced off the dirt and a great downpour followed only seconds later

Water streamed down Dylan's neck, back, legs and into his trainers. For a split second, he felt relieved. His hair clung to his head and his clothes stuck to his body, but at least he recognised rain. Rain, he was used to. It was airports, aeroplanes, cities and cars and dangerous people with guns that were terrifying. He tilted back his head and opened his mouth, swallowing drop after drop and feeling the splash on his eyelids and cheeks. For a few moments he was in the top field with Dad, heaving an injured sheep onto the quad bike, both of them soaked to the skin, but neither of them even mentioning the pouring rain.

Lightning cracked the sky in two and thunder followed a moment later. Dylan dashed under the balcony with all the butterfly cages. Silver streaks in the dark sky made the butterflies glow in technicolour. A lilac one with purple splodges splayed its wings out at full stretch. Here was another creature, stuck, just like him, in a place it didn't want to be. Dylan felt calmer, just looking at it. If he just kept thinking about the butterflies, he might be able to pretend the rest of the world had gone away. Another one, with folded wings, was see-through. An orange border framed the wings and there were black struts to support their shape, but the rest of the wings might have been made of glass. A third butterfly, brown and pale blue, threw itself against the cage bars, over and over.

The downpour stopped suddenly, as if a power shower in the skies had been turned off, and the dark clouds had found another part of the world to scowl at. Dylan came out from under the balcony and looked up. It was empty except for the guy whose arm still dangled between the railings, drips forming from his middle finger. Dylan shook himself, wet, but warm, the sun sinking into his shoulders. Damp patches on the mud shrank in the heat. The last of the rivulets slithered down into the open drain.

Dylan still had a sense of being watched from somewhere, but each time he swung round, wherever he looked, there was no one. Only the teenager, asleep with his mouth open, lay on the balcony and he definitely wasn't watching anyone.

So this would be the moment. He flipped open the latch and tilted the cage. The pale blue and brown butterfly came to the edge and launched itself into the air, weaving its way randomly off into the distance. Dylan flew with it for a while, felt the fresh air against its wings, its rush of energy as it fluttered upwards and away, until it disappeared into the blue. He opened another cage and another. He was still stuck, completely stuck, but each time a butterfly flew away, he felt a tiny bit freer, a tiny bit less panicked. He would have to run as soon as he had finished, he knew that. When he came to the last butterfly, it wouldn't go at all. Dylan didn't want to damage its wings by touching it, so he kept tilting the cage.

'Out you go,' he whispered.

'Pssst!'

One of the kids who had taken his rucksack beckoned to him urgently, his eyes wide. The kid dashed towards him, grabbed him by the wrist and dragged him along up an alley way, almost out of sight of the butterfly cages and the balcony.

The kid tapped his skull in a sign Dylan easily recognised. 'Loco!' he said. 'Stupid boy!'

'Wait! Where are you taking me?'

The kid pointed back towards the butterfly cages. A teen had come out onto the balcony. The kid pointed at Dylan and drew a sinister line across his own throat. His huge eyes blinked and his chin wobbled. Dylan looked back. The guy had leant over the balcony and noticed that a cage door was open. He ran down the steps and when he saw that all the butterflies – except one – had gone, he let out a huge roar and looked wildly around. Dylan's wrist was yanked again and he had no choice. He ran after the kid, taking turns up smaller and smaller paths between shelters, jumping over open drains and dodging dripping washing on lines.

They came to an enormous rubbish heap, a huge, sprawling hill of mangled mess. Twisted bits of metal, stained fabrics, large pieces of cracked plastic, sheets of soggy cardboard. Odd breeze blocks, splintered wooden poles. Everything was so broken and mixed up together, that you couldn't tell what any of it had once been.

At the dump in Mach, you could find useful things. Mum often came back after doing the recycling, delighted with some 50p bargain she had found. Some bowl that was just right to put under a pot plant, or a stool for her polytunnel. But this dump was just an abandoned mess. And it wasn't just one rubbish heap – the hills went on as far as Dylan could see, as if they had replaced normal, green ones. They even seemed to have their own valleys, with streams of dirty water running between them. Dylan followed the boy between the hills of waste, trying to avoid the dark water.

Perched in one of these valleys was a yellow bus. It had no wheels and all the windows were missing, but Dylan felt a bolt of hope shoot through him, just because it was so good to see something he could identify.

As they arrived, the kid yelled something and a howl went up and children sprouted from everywhere. One jumped off the roof onto a soggy mattress, did a roly-poly and leapt up again. The strange thing was, they all seemed to be dressed as if they were about to put on a performance of *Oliver Twist*. When Dylan had done this at primary school, everyone had borrowed their parents' gardening clothes, or some old jacket of their grandfather's, or clothes with holes in which their mothers were keeping for rags. None of these kids wore anything that fitted. Most of them didn't have shoes. In fact quite a lot of them were staring at Dylan's trainers. Dylan followed the kid as he picked his way through squashed plastic bottles to the front of the bus. The kid pushed Dylan up the steps, to where the door would have been, if there had been a door. A girl half-sat, half-lay, in the driving seat, chewing something and carving a tiny figure out of a small block of wood.

The kid gabbled something at her and her eyes grew wide. She sat up properly, spat the toothpick out of her mouth and asked a question. At the answer, she gazed at Dylan, slowly shaking her head. She asked him something.

'I don't speak your language,' he said.

The girl knelt up on her seat and turned round to the double seat behind her.

'Lucia!' she called to another girl, with shiny black hair in a loose ponytail down her back. As the girl looked up,

Dylan saw that she had a short tufted bit at the front which stood upright above her dark face and the bright whites to her serious brown eyes. A long-legged grey puppy lay on her lap, its huge paws – ten times too big for the rest of it – resting on her knees. Gradually, with one finger marking her place, the girl closed the fat paperback book she was holding. Between the book's tatty covers, the pages were grey and curled back on themselves so that it was twice as wide at the cut edges as it was at the spine. A short plastic bookmark lay in its pages, the sort that curls into a wristband if you snap it against your wrist.

'English?' she said, scrambling to sitting position, as if there was something exciting about speaking English.

'Welsh,' Dylan said.

'I am speaking English more superbly than Queen Victoria Becks,' said the girl, with quiet pride. 'Lucia,' she added, holding out her hand. 'Meaning light.' She reminded Dylan of Matt. She also had something slow and dark running in her veins. But it wasn't salty, like Marmite, it was rich and good and sweet, more like molasses. How odd to think of molasses twice in one day.

'Dylan,' he said.

Lucia's eyes narrowed.

'I am not familiar with such a name. What is meaning of name "Dylan"?'

Dylan shrugged. 'Dunno,' he said, which just made Lucia's eyes narrow further.

The first girl explained something in Portuguese.

'You are liberating butterflies?' Lucia asked. 'Man exterminate if he see you.'

'Yeah, I guessed he would be cross,' Dylan said. 'But what could he do, really?'

Lucia gaped at him and translated his words to the group, who drew back in horror. As if to illustrate, the first girl grabbed Dylan by the hair and pulled his head to one side. She lay her penknife flat against his neck, drew it slowly across, then showed him the sharp edge of the knife, scraping her thumb carefully against it. Dylan glanced at Lucia.

'Is act teenager perform,' confirmed Lucia, nodding.

Dylan swallowed. OK, so this place was poor and the people lived 'close to the ground' as his mum would say. But would the guy really have killed him? For setting butterflies free? He looked from face to face. Every single one was deadly serious, and these kids didn't look the sort to scare easily. His mouth went dry.

He was distracted by a bright yellow T-shirt – his T-shirt – on a kid.

'Hey, you're the gang who stole my rucksack,' he said. 'Give it back!'

Lucia smiled, translated, and the whole bus erupted with laughter.

'Geeve eet back!' they mimicked, clapping and leaping about. There was his hat and his spare shorts on another kid. The first girl was laughing so much she was losing control. She looked at Dylan's face and howled with laughter. She gasped for breath and tears rolled down her face.

'I don't see what's so funny,' he said. 'You shouldn't steal.'

Lucia recovered first and spoke over the laughter.

'If no stealing, we transform to bones. No nice Mama and Papa here. You learn to steal. I educate you.'

'I can't stay here. I have to get back to the city.'

'You have money to pay me to take you?'

'No, but…'

'You have family in Manaus?'

'No, but…'

'You think it safe for pretty boy like you in city?'

'Pretty? I'm not…'

Frantic calls and shouts could be heard coming closer and Dylan looked out of the window to see a boy about Tommo's age running up towards the bus. He was barefoot and wore only shorts and his face was smeared with something black. Panting, waving his arms around, speaking in bits of words, the boy managed to get a sentence out and Lucia whispered the translation with real fear in her eyes.

'Butterfly teenagers arrive to slaughter you most badly,' she said.

FIFTEEN

Lucia tipped the huge grey puppy off her lap and leapt out of her seat. She stuffed the book into her pocket, grabbed Dylan by the arm and shot out of the gap where the front door would have been.

'Wait – I have to have my passport and ticket. Keep the rucksack, just give me…'

Lucia screamed a translation and the first girl ruffled through the rucksack and threw them at him, yelling at him to go.

'Follow with excellent swiftness,' Lucia called behind her. She raced uphill, along a pathway between the ugly mess of waste with its gleaming lumps of wet plastic wrapping. Her puppy galloped beside her, long gangly legs bouncing along on great paws. After a while they came to a pile of rotting fruit. She stopped and picked through it fast, kicking and throwing things to one side and wiping her hands on her shorts. The smell was so sweet it made Dylan gag.

'Melon,' she said, holding up a large, dirty half melon. She broke it in quarters and began to chew at the clean, broken side.

'Thanks for rescuing me back there,' Dylan said, panting, and glad she didn't offer him any of the melon, even though he was hungry.

'Not rescue you. Dispose of you. Trouble for us guys if you stay with us. Teenagers won't leave if we keep you. I escort you to other gang.' The juice dribbled down her chin as she gnawed right up to the dirty edge, but managed not to let any of it touch her lips.

'Do you guys live in that bus?'

'Yes, we most fortunate.'

'With no adults at all? No school?'

'Adults not trustworthy. School a squander of time.'

'Squander?'

'Waste.'

'That's what I think,' Dylan said. 'Learning all sorts of rubbish you don't need.'

Lucia turned to him sharply.

'Learning is good. I learn every matter all the time. I need learn everything. I squander no time not learning. But quicker than in school. You go to school, right?'

'Yes,' admitted Dylan.

'But you no speak my language. I speak yours.' She

patted her pocket. 'I learn from anything I find. These rubbish dumps,' she waved an arm at the heaps either side of them, 'many writings here. Stories, instructions for washing machines, maps. I learn all. Off and on,' she glanced at him. 'You say "off and on", yes?'

'Er, yes.'

'Sometimes adults approach, strive to make us come toward their school, but I too extremely clever to trust them. You are not wanting to know what adults are thinking.'

'Some adults are alright,' Dylan said cautiously. Until he had met Anton there had never been an adult he didn't trust. Plenty who were extremely annoying, but none who were actually dangerous.

'So you guys live how you want, no adults, no school, no rules? We're all shut up in classrooms all day long. You're free all day?'

Lucia spat a melon pip on the ground.

'Free? These kids alright now. In five years, kids become teenagers on balcony. These kids are in worse cage.' She tapped her head. 'In here. They think impossible escape this place.'

'And you? You are going to get out of here?'

Lucia gazed off into the distance and fondled the puppy's ears. Then she turned to Dylan.

'You,' she said, pointing at him with surprising certainty, 'are conversing with future President of Brazil. I learn everything.' She patted the book in her pocket again. 'Here my thesaurus. I know more words than you do.'

'Is that why you speak like that? What is a thesaurus, anyway? It sounds like a dinosaur. Is it a dictionary?' Dylan reached out to her pocket, but Lucia jumped back and hissed at him.

'You no grasp my book!'

'I don't want your stupid phrasebook. I just wanted to look at it.'

'Not stupid phrasebook. Excellent clever dictionary and thesaurus. I have best words. Thesaurus hold words in groups in same meaning. So see "cold" and it tells you other excellent words similar. Best, best words. I speak English superior to you. I know more words in your language than you.'

'I don't think so.'

'How many words for cold you know?'

Dylan thought.

'Freezing, chilly. Nippy.' In the scorching heat the words seemed completely meaningless.

'Frigid, crisp, cool, wintry,' countered Lucia.

'Icy, shivery.'

'Gelid,' she said, triumphantly.

'Gelid? That's not a word.'

'So it is, see.' She opened the thesaurus and showed it to him. Dylan thought hard. He couldn't let this cleverclogs, as Gramp would call her, win.

'OK, parky,' he said.

She consulted her list.

'Parky not here,' she said. 'Incorrect. Bad word.'

'No, it's not. It's a sort of slang word.'

'Slang?'

Now he had got her. She didn't know about slang.

'Like not a proper word for dictionaries but everyone uses it and knows what it means.'

Lucia's face fell.

'You imply not all words in excellent thesaurus?' she demanded. 'If so I learn all entries, I continue not understand everything?'

Dylan shrugged. 'Fraid so.'

'Frayedsoh? What is that?'

'It's short for 'I am afraid so.'

'Why you are afraid?'

Dylan sighed. Did this girl never give up? 'I'm not afraid. It's just a saying. Like "I'm afraid to tell you that it is so". Or "I'm sorry to tell you that it is so". That sort of thing.'

'Fraid so,' repeated Lucia. A light flashed in her brown eyes. 'Yes. I require slang in addition. You will stay here in my favela. I discover you safe place from exterminator. You teach me your low slang.'

Stay. Dylan's brain was foggy with hunger and all the heat. It seemed harder and harder to remember what the most important thing was. Talking to Lucia was the best thing that had happened since they discovered Mac and Joe were missing, but there was something he had to do, wasn't there? He had to get back to the centre of Manaus to see the CEO.

'No, Lucia. I have to go. I need to get to the Manaus Opera House. I'll teach you slang if you take me.'

'The Opera House? You want to go sightseeings of Manaus?'

'No,' he said. He explained all about BlueBird, the CEO, his farm, the Annual General Meeting.

'You meet and converse with such a man?' Lucia's eyes were huge. 'You think he listen to you?'

'Yeah, grown-ups are a bit soft like that. I'll have to look him in the eye and talk straight, of course. That's the only way to do it.'

Lucia shook her head wonderingly. 'Grown-ups are soft where you come from?' She shrugged. 'OK, I convey you there. Lengthy distance to travel. You pay me with many slang words.' She thrust the puppy into Dylan's arms. 'Meet Pernickety – meaning 'careful with details'.' The long-limbed puppy greeted Dylan with a soft 'yaroo' and a wag. 'In my esteemed opinion an excellent name for a tremendous hound. But she is too infantly for a long run. You will transport Pernickety.'

Dylan grasped the young dog around its dangling legs and breathed in. Her strong warm puppy smell flooded his brain, as delicious and sweet as a mouthful of marshmallows, and for a moment he floated away on the sweetness, his eyes closed. Megs would be fast asleep at home, safe and warm and curled up in her basket, he felt sure of that. Tommo would be spoiling her and feeding her too many titbits. The thought of her beautiful, keen face and wagging tail made his throat gulp and his eyes sting. He couldn't hug Megs, but at least he could hug Pernickety until he got control of himself again.

Lucia took him on a roundabout run downhill out of the dump, down the track and back onto tarmac until they came to the small red-brick houses, some without windows, then the school and library and left the place behind them. Pernickety's weight doubled each time they turned a corner, and Dylan's arms ached. They jogged through back streets into a fruit market, where from one stall Lucia snatched a great lump of purple. Her hand moved so deftly, and her speed stayed so exactly the same that the stall holder didn't even notice. They shot around three more corners before she found a doorway and backed into it. The strange purple oval thing was halved expertly with her bendy ruler, which she licked clean and shoved back in her book. The inside was as purple as the outside and looked like old play-doh. She held a half in each hand.

'Learn me something,' she said, 'and I pay you with food.'

'Um, how about "Grub's up"?' Dylan said, his mouth watering. 'It means, food is ready.'

'Ha! Grubzup,' Lucia said, handing him half. 'Time is grubzup. Consume.'

'Or,' Dylan said, so hungry that he bit into the purple

play-doh without caring what it was, 'You could say, tuck in. Or stuff your face. Gobble up. Get your laughing gear around that. Wolf it down.' He swallowed. Whatever it was, it tasted familiar. 'What the heck is this?'

'Your … laughing … gear?' Lucia stared at him, then burst out laughing herself. 'Mouth!'

Her face as she understood made Dylan laugh too. 'Mouth? Gob. Chops. Cake-hole.'

'Cake-hole?' Lucia screamed with laughter.

'Oh!' Dylan yelled. 'It's a potato! It's a purple potato!'

'Of course potato,' Lucia said, looking at him as if he was stupid. 'Lengthy, lengthy gap still between us and Opera House,' she said, in a normal voice, then shrieked, 'Ay caramba!'

She shot across the road to two young men who were sitting on yellow motorbike taxis, looking at their phones. As Dylan watched, she whacked one of the men on the back, threw her arms up in the air and screamed at him. The man shook his head at her and showed her his watch, but she kept on yelling at him and hitting him. Then she turned to Dylan and beckoned him to come over.

'Have sight of my richly brother. He convey us to Opera House in grand luxury, similar to fancy business lady.'

The young man shouted at her, slipped his motorbike off its stand and drove away, leaving Lucia screaming behind him.

'Useless rotten brother! He experience much sorrow

when I become President of Brazil and he want favour.' Her eyes were blazing, but they were wet as well.

'Lucia, it's OK. We'll walk. I'll carry Pernickety.'

But they didn't have to. The young man on the other yellow TAXI motorbike tilted his head to indicate that they should get on the back of his bike.

'This courteous one is my brother's friend,' Lucia said quietly, blinking, and taking Pernickety from Dylan and burying her head behind the soft ears. 'He say he speak to my scurrilous brother most harshly one day. Come. Let's ascend on board.'

The young man pressed a button and the bike came to some sort of life, spluttering and coughing until it settled into a regular growl. Lucia climbed on the bike behind him with Pernickety in her arms, and signalled to Dylan to get on too and hold on to her waist, as she was holding on to the driver's.

As if from a great distance, a distance of around five thousand, five hundred and sixty eight miles, Dylan heard the faint voice of his mother saying 'Never go anywhere with anyone you don't know. Never go on a motorbike. Never go cycling on the road without your helmet.' Dylan hesitated. Why did breaking all of those rules feel like the safest thing he could possibly do?

'Don't stand there like palm tree,' Lucia yelled over the noise of the engine, so Dylan climbed on to the torn plastic seat behind her with his heart hammering in his throat.

They took off so fast that Dylan felt cool air blast over his face and through his hair. His body was pulled backwards as the driver zipped off, speeding along clear patches and overtaking and undertaking whenever there was a car in his way.

They shot past a man sitting by a wheelbarrow which overflowed with monster green bananas, watermelons and tiny oranges, turned left by a huge shop which sold only bras, hundreds and hundreds of them, and Dylan nearly tipped off the back when they took a right between two shops selling hammocks in butterfly-bright colours. The driver slowed down to wave at a man sitting at the edge of the pavement with a small table, a mirror, scissors, and a huge container of water, ready to cut people's hair. He yelled at a man in the middle of the road carrying a board showing before and after photos of a mouthful of teeth and braces. It was so warm and so noisy and busy and colourful that, for the first time in his life, Dylan enjoyed being in a city. He wanted this bike ride to go on forever, just him and Lucia swooping along busy streets, with Pernickety's nose stuck up in the warm air, sniffing, watching all the people shoot past.

But the bike slowed down. They had come to a large square with a monument in the middle. Grey and white cobblestones swirled around each other in a pattern. A huge pink building stood at one side of the square. It looked like a palace, with all the edges covered in white icing sugar. It had a funny green and yellow dome on top, which looked grand in a different sort of way, and ugly against the pink.

A large banner announced that the BlueBird conference began this afternoon with a talk by the CEO and went on for three more days. On the last day it said Projectos Especiais in bold. Special Projects. Golly, Portuguese really was easy. This was it. This was his chance. His heart battered about in his chest as he climbed off the motorbike.

'Hey, thanks,' he said to the young man, grinning madly. The ride had been better than a funfair. Lucia clambered off too and the man shoved his hand in his pocket, pulled out a scrappy piece of paper and gave it to Lucia. Then he kicked the bike stand and shot off across the square.

'Hey, he donate me two reals!' Lucia said, her mouth open, staring after the bike. 'And not even a brother!'

'Lucia, it's nearly time; it'll be starting. Thank you … for getting me here. Will you still be here when I've finished?' It started as a simple question, but halfway through he realised how much he wanted her to wait for him. Losing Floyd was bad enough, but losing Lucia suddenly felt terrifying.

'Oh, no,' she said, indignantly. 'You not go alone. I need learn all about palace behaviour and talking. I come too.'

Two uniformed Opera House attendants stood at the door, greeting people in suits as they entered the building. Dylan waited for a break in the stream of people, then approached the doormen. He told them that he had to see the CEO of BlueBird, but they shooed them away, one of them even kicked out a foot, like you would at a pigeon, or a stray dog, without even letting him finish. Dylan was stunned. Plenty of grown-ups had got cross with him, but they had always listened to him when he wanted to speak. Who did they think they were, treating him like some sort of pest? So much for grown-ups being soft.

They walked back down the wide steps in silence. Dylan's head was popping with ideas. Maybe they could wait for the CEO to come out? Maybe they could sneak in behind the doormen later? Maybe … Lucia nudged him.

'Suspect existence of a singing door,' she said.

What was she going on about now? Did she think an opera house actually sang?

'A singing door? Oh, a door for singers?'

'Precisely and exactly. A singing door.'

They ran round to the back of the building and did indeed find another door. It was locked. Lucia bent low and peered at the lock and shook her head.

'Not possible to unlock without key,' she said.

'Well, duh,' Dylan said, rolling his eyes.

'What is 'duh'?' asked Lucia coldly. She had clearly understood his tone, if not the word.

'It just means like, "that's obvious". Of course you can't unlock it without the key.'

'Under the contrary.'

'You mean sometimes you can?' Dylan asked.

'Certainly. Usually. With facility. But this one complicated.'

At that moment a man came out through the door and turned abruptly left. Cigarette and lighter came together, a brief flare and the man sucked on his cigarette, leaning back against the wall. The door, however, was on one of those slow close mechanisms and, seeing their opportunity, Dylan, Lucia and Pernickety snuck in, seconds before it smoothly brought itself to a clunking shut.

SIXTEEN

They ran up concrete steps to a thick red rope strung across the top step. They slipped under it and looked around. Ahead was a small shop, with carved wooden jaguars and sloths and parrots on keyrings. Behind them a smarter staircase of polished wood disappeared upwards.

Somewhere in this huge building the CEO was walking or talking or eating or looking out of a window but Dylan had no idea where. It was like playing one of those kiddy party games where people yell 'hotter' or 'colder' to tell you how close you are to finding the thimble, or whatever had been hidden. Pernickety's claws clicked uncertainly on the polished wood. You probably weren't supposed to bring dogs in here, Dylan thought, and picked her up.

Lucia looked grave.

'Essential find elevated terrain.'

'Find *what*?'

'Elev … higher ground. We go up, we look down. We have more understanding of building.' She ran off up the staircase with Dylan following her. It seemed the place was empty and yet Dylan had a sense of lots of people nearby. The squeaky sound of a microphone being tested and the shuffling of feet and loud polite laughter came from somewhere.

At the top of the stairs they came to a curved wall with several doors, equally spaced, leading to the centre of the building.

'Further up,' Lucia hissed, so Dylan heaved Pernickety into a more comfortable position and kept on going.

The next level had a stripey floor. Dark brown planks alternated with pale yellow wood. It reminded Dylan of something, but it seemed odd, in such a smart building. It was the sort of thing you would do if you didn't have enough money for a new floor but had bits left over that would do. Then he remembered: when he had been in the plane he had seen the two colours of the Amazon river, one dark brown, the other yellow.

'Hey, guess what they've done here,' he said, but Lucia wasn't listening.

Three faceless mannikins, clothed in rich velvet colours: blood red, midnight blue and a green so dark it was nearly black had caught her attention. The cloak in midnight blue had gold trimmings around it and clearly had some sort of magical power over Lucia. She had frozen in front of it, standing stock-still and it didn't look as if she would ever move again.

'Lucia, we can't stop. Someone will come.' The talk and laughter were growing louder. Dylan let Pernickety jump down and yanked Lucia's arm. 'Come on!' he whispered, and pulled her round the corner just as a door opened behind them and the voices – some English, some Portuguese, some something else – became properly audible.

'Lucia?' Her eyes had become round and still. 'What's the matter?'

'Cloak of glory blue,' she whispered. Then she shook herself. 'Come *on*, Dylan,' and she rushed up the next flight of stairs.

On the next curved corridor the doors leading to the centre of the Opera House were shutting and the noise of chairs shifting about could be heard.

'Up one solitary more staircase, I surmise,' Lucia said.

As they turned back towards the staircase Dylan had a horrible fright. Two ragged, scary-looking kids had been following them. Time stood still as Dylan took in their desperate faces, their dirty clothes, one barefoot, one with wrecked shoes and – what was that?

The moment Dylan saw their dog, he realised it was a huge mirror. That boy there, with fierce eyes and a streak of dirt down his face – that was him. And that girl, with determined brown eyes, with the loose ponytail and the short tufts that shot upwards from her forehead – that was Lucia. His heart sank. No wonder the doormen wouldn't listen to him. Dylan looked down at himself. His clothes were sticky with juice, and his trainers, even though most of the disgusting stuff had been washed off in the rain, were still a suspicious sort of brown and you could see that they might have started life another colour. His hair, which had never been tidy for a single day of his life, had just been blasted by wind on the motorbike. Mum would say he looked like a shocked lion. Would the CEO listen to him, looking like that? Would any grown-up listen to anyone so dirty?

They ran up the last staircase. Here, some of the doors leading into the curved wall were open. They entered one and closed it quietly behind them. The door led into a small enclosed balcony with four red velvet chairs, each with a piece of paper on. Dylan heard Lucia gasp behind him and looked over the balcony into the theatre. It was like being in a fairy tale palace. Rob would have loved it. Everything was either gold or red or pink or cream. Pale columns held up three tiers of balconies, all with the same red velvet chairs. The first level of columns had pink circles at the top, with names written on them. Was that actually Shakespeare written on one of them?

The chairs on the ground floor were full of people in suits and there was a hush as a man came on to the stage and tapped the microphone. 'Bom Dia' he said, and the words 'Good morning' flashed up on a long thin screen above his head. Then some strange beautiful shapes flickered across the screen – Chinese, perhaps.

He began to talk, and as he did, Dylan recognised him from the website. This was Mustafa Shadid, the CEO of BlueBird. This was the man he had come to meet, right there, with nothing between Dylan and him at all but a bit of air. What would he be like? What ran in his veins? Would he be the same as Miss Crassy and Anton? Dylan's throat clamped shut and he had to gasp to breathe. Mr Shadid began to speak in Portuguese, and his words flashed up on the screen in English on one side and in Chinese on the other.

'First I'd like to thank my friend for letting us use this stunning Opera House for the opening of our Annual General Conference.'

This was the man who had the power to change Dylan's life. The more Dylan knew about him and the more he understood him, the better chance he would have of persuading him to sell their farm back to them. Every word he spoke was a clue, a chance. Dylan didn't take his eyes off the screen.

'This has been an unusual year,' it said. 'We have found nearly a hundred more sites – all over the world – in which to experiment with natural products. On Thursday, the last day of our conference, we will have presentations from three regional special projects managers, as you will see from your agendas.' At this point everyone checked the piece of paper in their hands and nodded. 'One of these regional managers will then be chosen to take on the role of Global Head of Special Projects. That person will have the ability to set up field camps all over the world to develop our ideas and hopes for the future – however off-the-wall and fantastical.'

Dylan snatched up the piece of paper from the seat beside him. Again, it was divided into three languages: Portuguese, Chinese and English. It said who was talking about what on each day of the conference, and on the last day, Thursday – the day Miss Crassy had mentioned on the plane – it said there would be presentations by Miss Gupta, Mr Xueqin and Miss Crassy.

So that was what she wanted. To be Global Head of Special Projects. It wasn't luck that he had met her on the plane. It was because she was on her way to this conference. And it was why Mac had circled Thursday on his calendar on the wall.

Dylan looked down at the screen again. '...pride ourselves on taking nothing away and leaving nothing behind. No place in the world shall be harmed by our work on healthcare. We are tireless in revisiting old solutions which have been discarded. To give you just one example, moss, for instance...' here Dylan's heart missed a beat, then rushed to catch up again '...was widely used as a dressing during World War One, when there wasn't enough cotton wool to go round. Sphagnum moss is highly antiseptic and highly absorbent. We are planning several experimental areas around the world to propagate this moss and to harvest it. Cotton wool, of course, requires bleaching which causes untold damage to the environment.'

The clapping when the CEO said this was deafening.

'He'll come off the stage soon,' Dylan hissed. 'We have to get backstage and catch him before he joins everyone else.'

They ran down three flights of stairs, but couldn't see a way of reaching the wings of the stage.

'Wait, what is here?' Lucia drew back a red curtain and found a door. 'This will be the way, I have certainty,' she said. The door led into a plain black corridor. All the golds and creams and reds and velvets were forgotten here. It was difficult to see in the darkness, but Pernickety trotted along happily and they followed her, narrowly missing odd bits of stage furniture. They opened a door and saw a man with his back to them and large headphones over his ears, twiddling knobs on a large dashboard. They backed out again and tried another door.

It led them to the wings of the theatre. From the side view, Dylan saw how tall and strong-looking Mustafa Shadid was. Dylan gulped. His armpits prickled and his palms felt damp. The moment was nearly here. He just had to get it right, make him listen, tell him everything.

The CEO picked up his papers, lined them up and tapped the bottom edges against the podium. He raised a hand to acknowledge the applause, smiled, and – unbelievably – came straight towards Dylan.

But Dylan had clearly become invisible. Mustafa Shadid would have marched straight into him, if Dylan hadn't hopped out of the way.

'Sir!' Dylan called. Mr Shadid glanced back and strode on. 'Sir, please, can I talk to you?'

Mr Shadid stopped. 'You speak English?' he said, with a London accent. 'What on earth are you doing begging in the Opera House?' He turned to the assistant beside him. 'Get these kids out of here, for goodness sake and give them enough for a meal each.'

And in that moment Dylan knew that something surprising, something with the powerful natural sweetness of pineapple juice flowed in Mustafa Shadid's veins. He was a good man. Everything would be OK, he would understand. It made Dylan braver, sure he could keep trying without making him angry.

'I'm not begging sir! My farm is one of the farms BlueBird has bought to prop... grow moss. But it wasn't really for sale.'

'What? Nonsense. Be off with you, lad.'

'No, Sir, wait, please, I am begging you, but not for money. Just to listen! My dad's a farmer and you've bought our farm. We want to buy it back.'

Now Mr Shadid sighed. He looked at his watch. 'You have exactly one minute to explain yourself.'

Dylan took a deep breath, looked him in the eye, and talked straight. He explained that BlueBird had bought their farm in Wales, that his family had farmed there for generations, that his whole life was supposed to be farming there, living in the village, growing up with all his mates. He described his dad, the pedigree sheep, saving up for the deposit to buy the land off the landowners, who had promised to sell it only to them. He said there was a farm in the next village that hadn't sold for months. The CEO began to frown. Dylan thought maybe he hadn't included enough about how much he loved the farm. He talked about the river and his plan to build a treehouse with his friends, build it himself, without grown-up help. Eventually he stopped. It seemed that the more he said, the more Mr Shadid frowned. There was a silence. He needed to say something that would really make him care. And then he remembered. Why was he talking about the farm when Floyd and Mac and Joe were in danger? He had got it all the wrong way round. 'And my friend is in danger and Miss Crassy just tried to get rid of me by having me left near the...' He stopped and looked at Lucia. It might rude to call her home the dump.

'The dump,' she said. 'Where I appropriate him.'

Then Mr Shadid stood up.

'Did she indeed,' he said, drily. 'How on earth did you get Miss Crassy's name? Now I know you're up to something.' He turned to Lucia. 'And what have you come for? I suppose you want something too?'

Lucia shrugged. 'Nought,' she said. Then her face brightened. 'Excepting cloak of glory blue on second floor.'

'Cloak of…?' Mr Shadid made an exasperated noise and turned back to Dylan.

'I don't know where you got your story from. But let's for a moment pretend it's true. This is what I would say to you: there's a bigger picture. And you're not seeing it. All you're seeing is your own life and what you want. There are bigger challenges, global ones. Try thinking about them sometimes and your own problems won't worry you quite so much. Everyone at BlueBird is dedicated to addressing these challenges with brilliant new ideas. I'm sorry that doesn't suit your plans perfectly, and that you – or whoever put you up to this – may not be able to build your treehouse, but I have work to do. Thank you for your time.' With extreme politeness, he bowed his head and walked away.

SEVENTEEN

Stunned, Dylan stumbled after Lucia as they were hustled down some back steps and out of the building. He followed her stupidly along a side street to a doorway in the shade, where Pernickety lay down and fell asleep.

It was all over.

Dimly aware of Lucia beside him, leafing through her book and muttering, Dylan dropped his head into his hands and hid in the darkness. A vision of the farm, the river, the rushing water appeared before his closed eyelids, huge and real, as big as a cinema screen. He could see details: the sparkling flowers of white water, the bright green moss on the fallen tree, the chirpy robin with his brown coat, red chest, grey blue underbelly and needle-thin legs. Then the picture broke up, crumbled like a jigsaw. Each piece broke into smaller ones and fell in a heap, like so many pixels, to the bottom of his mental screen. He would not grow up on the farm. He would never shear his own sheep in the shed, spend his days on the quadbike in the fields with Megs, or one of her puppies, or grandpuppies, helping get the sheep in.

Then he realised that that wasn't even the worst part of it. The worst bit was that he wouldn't grow up with Matt and Aled and Rob and Floyd. They would still sit on the fallen tree after school every day, telling each other stories, pretending to push each other off, maybe coming up with their own ideas for things to build in the woods and around the farm. And he would be alone in town, one of those teenagers who wandered around the streets in small groups eating chips, trying to look cool but actually looking pointless, hanging around the playground like giant babies who couldn't work out what to do now they were big. It hurt so much. He didn't feel angry and determined any more. He felt a huge sadness that he knew would last a very long time. Matt would probably invite him over at weekends, and Dylan would try to join in, but he would feel separate and different and after a couple of weekends he would never go again. And he knew he wasn't being overdramatic about this. That was exactly how it would be.

Ever since he had heard his dad say the word 'sold', Dylan had been outraged, sure he wouldn't know who he was if he wasn't growing up at home, on the farm, in the village, with Matt and Aled and Rob. Now he had to face it.

All those things would go. Did that mean that he wasn't a person anymore?

'Teach more slang,' Lucia said, nudging him. 'If mouth equals gob, tell me ears?'

There was a long silence.

'Lugholes,' Dylan said, through his fingers. With a huge effort he dropped his hands and stared at the swirly black and white cobblestones at his feet. 'How could you ask for a cloak?' he asked.

'No necessaries becoming crossy with me. You arrange your messy, you sit in it.'

'Thanks, Lucia. That's sweet.'

A business woman in a smart suit and shiny black shoes came marching along the pavement. She was munching an apple, taking big bites at first, then smaller ones, twisting it round and round to get all the last bits off it, as if it was a job she needed to do really well. She crossed the road and flung the skinny apple core away. It fell into the gutter and rolled towards a drain. Dylan watched it roll until it came to a stop, right over the drain. One squish and it would be through. That was exactly what he felt like: an apple with all the flesh stripped off. Nothing left except the core and few seeds.

The question was, what was left of him? Who was he when everything was taken away? And as soon as he asked himself the question, the answer came, as if by magic, and he understood that if he had never had to ask the question, he would never have known the answer. What he had in his core were ideas. He always had a plan of some sort, a solution, a way to try and get round things.

Last summer, his plan to build the bike track had fallen to bits, so he had decided to earn enough to buy a bike instead. Then, when he had enough money, he had changed his mind and decided to buy and train Megs. And strangely it had all ended up with building the bike track anyway. Dylan never minded plans changing, though giving up trying to save the farm was more painful than anything he had ever given up before. It was not having a plan at all, not having any idea what to do next, that made him feel like a chucked-away apple core.

So he had a think. If the most painful part of losing the farm was losing his friends, and if Floyd – who he still hoped would turn into a good friend if he ever found Joe and melted a bit – was upriver somewhere, in danger, then maybe that was what he should do next.

But how? The piece of paper on Miss Crassy's seat on the plane was easy to remember. MED5 it had said. Manaus Eastern Docks 5.

It would mean finding the boat taking the supplies upriver. It would mean hiding on the boat with Miss Crassy's men – maybe Anton – and going up the Amazon.

He pictured himself hiding, scrunched up somewhere on the boat, and his gut lurched. He swallowed back a wave of fear in his throat. But what else could he do? He had no money to get back to Salvador and anyway he couldn't leave Floyd. Hang about in Manaus hoping someone would come and save him? How could that possibly work? If he didn't come up with a plan, any sort of plan, and make it happen, he wouldn't be himself. He wouldn't be anyone at all.

He wished Matt was with him to help him work out what to do. Matt and Aled and Rob would be in the dormitory with all the rest of Years 7 and 8, probably messing around at some game. His stomach ached to think of them all laughing at each other's pyjamas, calling each other names. Such a hot feeling swept through him that he had to blink a few times. He took some deep breaths and cleared his throat, to make sure his voice sounded strong.

'Lucia? I'll teach you more slang if you take me to the docks.'

On the way he explained about Miss Crassy and Anton and Floyd and Joe and Mac.

'Plausibly Anton annihilate you,' she said, thoughtfully.

'Annihilate?' Dylan stopped and turned to face her, suddenly furious with her stupid words. 'Annihilate? Why don't you just say "kill" ?' He glared at her. 'Obviously I don't think anything bad could possibly happen to me or my friend, do I? So say it straight. You sound bonkers using all these big words.'

'Bonkers?'

'Mad.'

'Why mad to utilise big words?'

Dylan's temper snapped. 'Big words might be OK in books, but you just sound like an idiot.'

Lucia spoke with great dignity. 'You speak about register. High register words are strong, important words powerful people use. Gelid. Your words are low register. Parky. I have much interest in both. I recommend wide interest.' She sniffed. 'It will be my rapture escorting you to docks.' She squeezed her thesaurus into a torn pocket and scooped up Pernickety. 'Speedy up,' Lucia said, scampering off down a side street.

She took him to a covered area with red roofs. They ran between aisles of tiny stalls, all selling hundreds and hundreds of useless things, all to do with having a nice, ordinary time. Did people really want all these woven fans and baskets, hats and flipflops, hammocks, beads and necklaces? Did they need so many different coloured powders to spice up their foods? So many dried herbs and roots and weird plants? Even if Dylan had had any money, there was nothing in the whole market which could have helped him find Floyd and get home again. They raced through the fish market where silver, pink, orange and gun-metal grey bodies shone on beds of ice as if anyone could care which sort of fish they ate. What a luxury, he thought, to have that sort of worry, when he had to find a boat, possibly with Miss Crassy's men on, and hide on it.

At last they came out onto a huge concrete expanse. It was the docks, the bank of the Amazon River, but you could hardly see the river for all the boats. Dozens and dozens of boats, as far as the eye could see.

Most of them were large, with four storeys all open to

the air and hung with hammocks close together. They were painted red and white, or blue and white and were crammed with people. On the lowest deck, nearest the water, massive boxes with pictures of potatoes on the side or huge bags of carrots were stored. More food was being loaded from the back of lorries at the dock's edge. Piles of bananas were everywhere. Dylan grabbed a loose banana from a wheelbarrow and ran off along the dock, peeling it. Others looked like day boats – smaller, with roofs to keep the sun off, but also open at all sides. Further along were boats that weren't designed for passengers, with large boxes or wrapped items loaded on to the deck.

Dylan looked for clues to see which one might belong to BlueBird. None of them had the name painted in large letters along the side, that was for sure. He came to a large cargo boat with a cabin at the front, and a great canvas covering the whole of the back, stretched high over something big. Two men were pulling the last corner of the canvas down to the hooks on the side of the boat. Dylan rushed to see what was being covered, and glimpsed the unmistakeable caterpillar treads of a digger. What was the first thing on the list on Miss Crassy's seat? Digger: 1. And how many diggers were likely to be going up the Amazon river today?

A muscly man pushing an empty wheelbarrow away from the boat noticed Dylan crouching down and frowned. He wore an oily T-shirt and combat trousers and his chin was dark with bristles. Then he saw Pernickety and his frown turned to a nasty grin. He was gazing at her as if she was the most interesting puppy he had ever seen. He muttered something which sounded as if it had 'Crassy' in it. He made a lunge for Pernickety, got a massive hand on the ruff of her neck and lifted her off the ground. Lucia screamed at him and Pernickety wriggled so hard that the man dropped her again. She scooted round between Lucia's legs and quivered there. The man hesitated, then turned back to his wheelbarrow and strode off.

'What was that about? Why would a man like that want a puppy? Did he say Crassy? He knew her name, didn't he?'

Lucia nodded, stroking Pernickety fiercely.

'So it's this one. I'm going to have to unhook it somewhere and climb in,' Dylan said quietly. He wished someone would say very loudly, "no, you're not, you're going to stand right there and in two seconds Floyd and Mac and Joe will appear in front of you, with tickets back to Salvador". It was the worst idea he had ever had. He was so scared he could feel his guts dissolving.

'Man departing to office. Momentous now.'

The canvas had been pulled so taut that it seemed impossible to unhook it. But Dylan grabbed hold of the edge and, with Lucia's help, pulled with all his weight. Millimetre by millimetre, the metal eye came down towards the tip of the hook.

'Yank it when I say three,' said Dylan, and, on three, they both yanked down and the eye scraped down under the hook and up again. A small flappy hole appeared, just big enough for Dylan to scramble through into the blackness.

'I'm in!' he whispered, his heart hammering away. He felt dizzy and sick. He wished Matt was with him, then he was glad he wasn't. Matt could always tell when Dylan was frightened, and right now he was plain terrified. He turned round and nearly scrabbled right out again. He gulped. 'Lucia?'

'Yes?'

'Nothing. Um. Nothing. Thank you.'

'Wait, tell me new low register word!'

If Dylan had had his hands near her neck, he would have strangled her. He both hated her and loved her for having no idea that he was more scared than he had ever been in his whole life. And considering everything else that had happened today, that was saying quite a lot.

'Cruddy,' he said, his voice wobbling. 'It means as horrible as the dried top of a cowpat.'

Through the small hole in the canvas, Dylan saw Lucia grin. 'Super word. I not forget you, Dylan,' and she disappeared.

Apart from a small amount of light coming from where they had loosened the canvas, it was completely black inside. There was hardly any space to move between packages and bulky objects. Hard angles pushed against Dylan's thigh, and he had already knocked his head against something with metal teeth.

He edged and bumped past various odd shapes until he

found a bit of space closer to the front of the boat. He sat with his knees up, hugging them. By the time he got out of here, he would be at the fieldcamp, with Floyd. He waited, his guts heaving with breaths as loud as thunder. Heavy footsteps made the boat tip to one side before the cabin door was slammed shut.

A male voice – that Dylan immediately recognised as Anton's – gave an order. There was a scuffling sound, then Lucia's furious voice, screaming and yelling in a mixture of languages, came clearly through the canvas.

'Frite em inferno! Fry in hell!' she screamed at one point, then 'Pernickety! Return to me my dog, idiota de merda!'

Lucia's yelling went on and on, interspersed with Anton's calm creamy voice and another man's, shouting. Then there was the sound of a slap and Lucia's screaming stopped dead.

Dylan sat up and banged his head. He had to get off. No, he had to stay on to find Floyd. He squeezed and crawled and scraped and knocked his way back towards the flap where he had climbed in. But before he got there, the engine fired up and the boat's hull vibrated under him. He was too late. He would never know what had happened to Lucia. The boat rumbled forwards slowly, still gently bumping the dock, then came to a halt. The horn blared, the engine revved and they were off.

EIGHTEEN

Above the deep hum of the engine, Dylan could hear thumping and banging sounds from the back of the boat, from the place where he had crawled in under the flap. 'Ay caramba! Santa Maria!'

'Lucia?' Dylan whispered, knowing he couldn't be heard. 'Is that you? Are you OK?'

Soft banging noises came closer and closer and at last two brown eyes appeared in the gloom.

'Greetings again,' she whispered back. 'I travel with you, guy.'

'Hey, thanks!' Dylan said, then cringed as she put her hand over his mouth. She was right, his voice had seemed insanely loud. They froze and waited. If they were caught now, it would all be over. As the noises carried on, Lucia shook her head.

'No,' she whispered. 'Not kindness. My youthful dog, they take him. I voyage with you, I retrieve him straight away, I return.'

'They took Pernickety?' His brain couldn't compute this information. What would the huge muscly man, or Anton, want with a puppy? The photo on Mac's wall of a lost-looking puppy and 'Stray Dogs?' written underneath it came to mind. 'Why did he do that?' he mouthed, with a nasty feeling growing in his gut.

Even in the darkness under the canvas, Dylan could see the look Lucia gave him.

'After he slap my face, I not enquire, "excuse me but inform me why you have stolen my dog". Foolish me,' she hissed.

The boat's engines roared and water churned and splashed at the stern. Then the boat changed direction and the engines settled back into their constant hum.

'Rotten uncomfortable place you choose. I discover better,' Lucia said, and crawled away.

Large, irregular shapes were appearing in the gloom. Pinpricks of light made their way through the canvas where there was a small tear, or an eyehole for a hook. Slowly he made out some sort of window.

'Psst!' Lucia hissed, above the hum of the engine. 'Here! I discover throne.'

Throne? What could Lucia mean now? Dylan knelt up and felt a sharp object poke him in the side.

'Ow!' A large wooden chest was blocking his way, but

he managed to climb over it. 'There's so much to bump yourself on here. Ow, my shin!'

Dylan recognised the sweet smell of new rubber from the day his dad's new tractor arrived last Easter. He came to enormous, thick black caterpillar treads, from which came a very faint shine.

'They must have serious mud where we're going,' Dylan muttered, clambering up and opening the digger door. It was much larger than his dad's and inside it had that new, bubblegum smell. The last time he had been in a digger, it had been his dad's and he'd driven it across a field with hay bales in the bucket while his dad shot past on his quadbike. It made him feel both better and worse to be inside a digger, here, on the other side of the world. Lucia's face appeared in the dimness.

'Sit next here. Excellent cosy. Close door so voices not heard.'

She sat on the large, well-padded driver's seat. The throne.

'Thanks.' Dylan shared the seat with her, edging halfway up the side. It would have been embarrassing to sit this close to a girl at school, but here it was OK. In fact it was more than OK. It was much better than being on his own in the dark.

'My dad's digger's seat is metal. This one's got suspension, hasn't it?' he said, bouncing a little in the seat.

'Teach suspension.'

'You know, it goes up and down if you go over a bump. So you don't feel it. It absorbs the bumps in the road. Or field. This must be brand new.' Dylan's fingers surfed over the familiar front levers, the ones at each side and the ignition switch behind him on the right. But what was this switch? Dylan flicked it.

Suddenly the cab was filled with light.

'Caramba! Extinguish the light!'

'Why?'

'Visible to see through canvas. Night time nearly now.'

Dylan could hardly bear to turn it off. The cabin gleamed with green and cream paint. The levers were all shiny black, unmarked. Dylan turned the light off, but the negative of what he had seen stayed in his eyes.

'Have you ever been in a digger before?' he asked Lucia.

'No.'

'Usually they're dirty, muddy machines with thick dust all over everything. They smell of manure, or engine grease. There's hay and tools and cloths and Dad's smokey bacon crisp packets lying around everywhere. This one – this is like a giant toy, all scrubbed and clean and shiny. And it's huge. Someone has spent a lot on this digger. My dad would bite your hand off if you offered him a digger like this.' He rested a hand on the ignition, and for a spilt second, he was home. 'I can drive this,' he said, a little shyly.

Lucia turned to him and gripped his wrist.

'You know driving this one? Teach me!'

Dylan laughed. 'Really? You want to learn everything? OK. Give me your hand.' He leant across her. 'Feel this key? That's the ignition. You turn that and the engine comes on. Feel these two levers in front?' He guided her hands to the two tall thin upright levers, only a centimetre apart. 'Push these forwards and it'll go forwards. Pull them back and it goes backwards.'

'So easy?'

'Yes. If you want to go right, you push the right one forwards and the digger turns right. Same for the left.'

'And the brake?'

'No brake. Just let the two levers come back to the normal position.

'Is same to your papa's digger?'

'Digger controls are the same all over the world.' It was one of Gramp's favourite rants. If farmers all over the world can agree on one set of digger controls, why can't politicians agree on one way of running a country? Then he would jab you in the shoulder with a gnarled finger. Because they get more money and jobs by disagreeing, that's why.

'And these other levers?' She was waggling a lever to her right.

'You won't need to learn those. They control the bucket.'

'Teach bucket control.'

'Why? You won't be driving a digger when you're president.'

'I learn everything. When I grow up you not discover me selling fish. I learn English perfection, driving digger, instructions for plumbing dishwasher, everything.'

Dylan was impressed. He had never imagined a girl could be interested in farm machinery. Maybe more of them would be if they had the chance. 'OK. The one on the right makes the bucket open or close or go up or down, and the one on the left swings the whole arm from left to right. But why do you want to fill your head up with all this stuff? What if you never need it? What about physics? You'll never need physics.'

Lucia spoke slowly and Dylan could just see her face. For once, it wasn't defiant.

'I need chances. Learning manufactures luck for me.'

Dylan grunted. 'I hate school. Hell on wheels, school is.'

To his surprise, Lucia agreed. 'I hate school. Evil people there.'

She sounded as if she hated it even more than he did.

'Evil? Have you ever been in a school?'

'Yes. Men who stink of beer. Games of chase you can't win. Not allowed out. Have to drink beer too. Have to wear dresses and grown-up clicky shoes. They give you the crazy pill. For free the first few times. It produce great happiness. But not real. Bigger sadness after. But you adore so much you needy have more. Then they make you pay. They seem nice when they come. Seem excellent trustworthy, but I no distinguish the difference. So I not trust any. They say big chance to learn English but I learn English better in solitude with thesaurus.'

'That doesn't sound like a real school,' Dylan said, frowning. 'School is awful, but it's clean. I mean, grown-ups force you to read books on every subject, history, geography, the sciences. They make you sit inside all day, but they do give you lunch and explain stuff. No one is ever allowed beer at school, not even the grown-ups.'

'They give you lunch?' Lucia's voice went soft.

'Every day.'

'They teach engineering?'

'Probably. You'd have to do loads of maths first.'

'I have seen such a school, in the entrance to my community, near the petrol station.'

'So why don't you go in? Ask them to teach you?'

'No place for street kid. If you no have address and no parent, consequently no place for you in nice school.' Lucia's eyes narrowed. 'What you have to do to get this nice place in your country?'

'You have to do all the homework. You have to go every single day. And be on time.'

'So simple? No beer? Wear high-heeled shoes like a grown lady?'

It sounded like such a strange school. Girls were forbidden to wear high heels in Machynlleth Secondary School. Dylan felt sad for her.

'No. But you do have to wear a uniform.'

'A uniform?' He couldn't see her eyes, but he could

hear her voice light up. She settled herself back in the seat.

'Dylan?' She said, quietly, 'We are not frightening, Dylan?'

Dylan was glad she couldn't see his face. He was even more glad that she was right there with him.

'No, Lucia,' he said, 'we are not frightened. We will find Pernickety and my friend and his family and then we will go home.' He swallowed. The thudding in his heart and ears and the panic that rushed through him must have been silent and invisible because she nodded.

'Excellent intention,' she said.

It wasn't an alarm clock, but it was something alarming that woke Dylan. Some noise, but all he could hear was the engine. He listened.

'Lucia,' he shook her awake. 'The engine noise has changed. It's deeper. That means it's slowing down. If they unload the boat straight away we'll be caught. Unless we can get inside one of these boxes or something.'

She was instantly awake. 'We discover hiding somewhere.'

They both slid out of the digger cabin and crawled and edged their way between obstacles under the canvas.

They found plenty of containers, but they were all sealed.

'What's that at the back there?'

'Cardboard boxes. Good to make home in. But flat now. No hiding spaces.'

'They'll have to do.'

They scrunched themselves up behind the flattened cardboard boxes and listened to the engine go deeper and deeper as it slowed. A soft bump, and the boat came to a halt. Doors slammed, rope flopped heavily on deck and men's voices could be heard calling to each other from every direction. Pernickety's 'yaroo!' made Lucia jump, then quickly settle down again. The canvas shook and the boat rocked.

'Unloading now. No chance to get off,' hissed Lucia.

'I think there are three men. One of them is Anton.'

They shrank down behind the packaging and kept still, hardly daring to breathe. Dylan moved his bruised legs carefully. Through neat finger holes in the cardboard Dylan watched dark figures peeling the canvas off all the awkwardly shaped objects. From their outlines, he could see Anton bossing the other two about. A sharp sting shot through his gut, like lemon juice on a cut.

The boat tilted as the men stood first on one side and then on the other. A scraping sound tore at his ears as the heavy boxes were pulled away. With a dull thump in his heart, Dylan saw that there was nothing but the digger and the cardboard left to clear away.

The men stood around the digger, their voices sounding as if they were discussing its features, and praising it. Then Anton's voice interrupted them with a direct order. Just hearing his voice made Dylan's body turn to concrete. There was nothing he could do but wait. He wondered how Lucia was feeling and was sure she would put up a fight.

Even breathing seemed to be an enormous upheaval under the cardboard. Both shins ached and his nose itched, but he wasn't going to risk scratching it.

Wait! The men seemed to be walking away. There was more laughter, the sounds of people who have finished a long job – or was that just wishful thinking? Then he heard shuffling coming towards him, soft movements, as if someone was trying to surprise him. Dylan closed his eyes as the cardboard was whipped off him.

Lucia stood above him, grinning.

'All fortunate, Dylan. Men departed.'

NINETEEN

Dylan sat up.

The last time he had seen the dawn, he'd been thousands of metres up in the air. Yesterday, in fact. And it was only two days since day had broken, dark red under a charcoal sky, over the car park in Machynlleth Secondary School. Now, above the dense green, a pale blue line was appearing in the sky. It was comforting, in a way. Proved he was on the same planet at least. Except that if he was taking comfort from the fact that he was still on planet earth, he must be in what Gramp would call a right pickle.

The boat was moored to a stake by a dirt clearing about the size of a football pitch, surrounded by a fence and thick tangled greenery. Three long wooden sheds were backed up against the long left-hand side of the fence, leaving half the space empty except for a few pallets and logpiles. The fence ran all the way round and back to the river bank again, except at the far end, beside the third hut, where it was hidden by a large piece of boarding. It was smaller than he had expected, this fieldcamp. It was the place Mac's walls had been screaming 'BLOODY MURDER' about, but it looked tidy. It wouldn't take long to find Joe and Floyd and Mac in a place this size. He would just have to get them away from Miss Crassy long enough to warn them about her. Beyond the fence was the Amazonian rainforest: Dylan could feel its rich intensity and hear it humming from where he sat. It was hotter here, off the river, and the air felt damp to breathe.

Behind him, a dark waterway led off towards the Amazon, but the Amazon itself was hidden by the heavy leaves and branches overhanging the creek. Also tied up against the bank were a small motor boat and a tree trunk, which had been partly hollowed out to form a rough canoe.

Anton and the two other men disappeared through the door of the furthest hut.

Dylan and Lucia looked at each other and nodded. They scrambled to the edge of the boat, where dark waters lay between them and the riverbank. Dylan was just about to tell Lucia to watch him and copy, when Lucia leapt over the gap first. They shot off towards the nearest hut, crouching as they ran, like evil cowboys in one of Gramp's old Westerns.

They slipped into the narrow gap between the hut and the fence. If the wire fencing was there to keep the jungle back, it wasn't succeeding. Thin green tendrils slipped in between the gaps making the fence bulge forwards, and the tendrils were followed by thick creepers, woody branches, huge flappy leaves on thin stems. Dylan breathed in a sharp clean smell of fresh leaves, and under that a rich and old smell, like a thick carpet of branches rotting under rainfall. There was also, sometimes, a sweet smell of sap, where a branch had broken off, revealing a pale interior. They squeezed past three large bins which stood side by side, each one with a picture of what should be recycled into it.

Stepping over branches, or crouching under them, they followed the length of the hut until they came to a window. Lucia put a hand on Dylan's arm.

'I'll look,' she said. 'If I am visibled and caught they won't know you are existing. First rule in favela: never let them know how many you are.'

She inched her head up over the window sill.

'What can you see?' hissed Dylan.

'Look.'

Dylan stood up straight. It was like Mum's strawberry polytunnel, but a fantasy version of it. A very tall man in a white coat was watering rows and rows of pots, each one labelled with paper tags. Purple shoots wound their way out of some of the pots, each one with a tight black bud the size of a fist at the end of it. Other pots had bushes with scarlet, star-shaped flowers, and out of others dripped long green fronds, all curling up at the edges, like fingers beckoning them to come closer. At least Dylan recognised what was on the furthest table: fully grown ferns, uncurled, reaching elegantly upwards, proudly displaying their complicated patterns on green arms. A sign in three languages said 'Take nothing that hasn't been authorised. Leave nothing behind. Every item must be recycled in the proper way.' This was just a greenhouse. Mac had been imagining things. Miss Crassy had been right about one thing – Mac was ill. He felt sad for Floyd.

'No Pernickety here,' Lucia said. 'Try next hut.'

The jungle seemed to reach through the fence to draw them in as they squeezed past the back of the first hut towards the second.

'Peculiar forms,' said Lucia, peering in. 'Limbs of machinery. Disintegrated tractor. Saws, wheels, chains. Appears a storehouse for broken things. Pernickety possibly existing here.'

'No food, then,' Dylan said gloomily. It was a very long time since the banana and the purple potato. 'Unless you're the Iron Giant.'

'Iron Giant?'

'Just a story.' Dylan caught up with her and looked in as well. He nearly whistled. 'My dad would love this. You could build anything in the world with all this stuff. Your own customised tractor. A new invention. Anything.'

The far wall was covered in garden stuff: thick twine, giant secateurs, shears, a massive scythe. 'But everything's too big. It makes me feel as if I'm about six again.'

'False teeth for crocodiles over there.'

'Might be for a chainsaw. A giant chainsaw.' The teeth and chain were so many times bigger than Dylan's dad's chainsaw. He tried to imagine the size of a man who could hold such a monster chainsaw and cut down trees with it. 'But it would be too heavy. No one could carry a thing like that.' I hope, he thought. A tapping on his shoulder made him jump and a small howl escaped him.

'Silence!' hissed Lucia. 'What is mattering?'

Dylan looked behind him and saw only a long branch which pushed through the wire fencing and dipped up and down as if some creature were dancing on it back in the dense greenery beyond the fence.

'Listen,' Dylan said. Strange noises told them there was life back there, rustling, fluttering, plopping, making grunts and squawks as creatures moved about.

'Necessary enter,' Lucia said, moving towards the front of the hut. 'Pernickety possibly here. Then I can go.'

'Go? We can't go until we find Floyd and Joe and Mac.'

'These men dangerous. I abscond as soon as I achieve Pernickety.' She clambered over a thick creeper and ducked under an overhanging branch.

'Wait.' Dylan pulled on her arm. 'You don't mean that. You can't leave as soon as you've got Pernickety. We all have to leave together. We're safer if we stick together.'

'Unlikely world you live in. Safer to be alone. No one harm you then.'

Dylan sighed and followed her towards the front of the hut. How could someone with such rich, dark treacle in their veins, something so good and strong, think something like that? That wasn't who she was. She must have got her thinking muddled up somehow.

'You can't just "go" anyway. How would you leave?'

'In canoe. Downstream to Manaus. No large dilemma.'

'Dilemma?'

'Problem. I consider it necessary you learn your language. Look – food!'

Through the window closest to the front of the hut they could see cages and food. So much food. Shelves and shelves of tinned food. Too much food for just a handful of people. Enough for dozens of people, for a long time.

Voices could be heard coming from the third hut. Lucia flattened herself against the wall and hissed at him to do the same.

Anton and his two men came out and shouted at each other. After a while they came into sight, pulling a wide, wheeled ramp towards the boat. Anton unbolted a section of the side of the boat and lay it flat, so the ramp could reach over the creek to the boat's edge. One man jumped on board and climbed into the digger, turned the engine on and swivelled it round so that its treads were in line with the ramp. With their backs to the hut, Anton and the other man watched him working.

'This is our chance, Lucia. Only the digger driver is facing our way and he's concentrating on not driving into the drink. Let's go.' Dylan and Lucia dashed round to the front of the second hut and slipped in through the door.

Rows of tinned food faced them. Baked beans, sweetcorn – hot dogs! Dylan's stomach shrink-wrapped itself around his spine. He wandered up an aisle, stroking the tins, stunned by the amount of food to choose from. He had just noticed another aisle, with hundreds of tins of dog food on, when a rattling noise came from the back of the hut. Lucia grabbed the two nearest tins and ran off towards the side wall. Dylan did the same and they both slipped behind a shelf just as the clattering noise became a roar of fury. From behind the shelves, a man came into view.

Wild hair sprang out in greying clusters from his head and his eyes bulged and darted about. A large black camera with a zoom lens dangled from his neck. He wore a dirty blue T-shirt, long sandy-coloured shorts and thick socks which bulged with papers sticking out of them. The man ranged from one side to another, a chain clanking at his heels as he moved.

'Come out, you scum! When I get hold of you you'll wish you hadn't lived to see this day. I know you're there. You think I can't hear you?'

He would see them in just a few seconds. Lucia clutched at Dylan's sleeve, catching a bit of flesh and pinching it. Dylan opened his mouth wide but managed to stop any sound coming out.

The man muttered to himself, looking this way and that, searching for them. Dylan's bones turned to glass as the man came round the last corner. Seeing Dylan and Lucia between the shelves, he stopped short at the end of his chain.

'Uh,' he said. Then he exploded. His arms shot up in the air and he ran from side to side, as far as his chain would let him, gabbling. 'Get out of here! Speak English? They are evil, they will destroy you. Is it Thursday? They are trying to kill me, kill my son, kill all the beautiful animals, before I can make the world believe me.'

The strange thing was, although this man looked madder and much more dangerous than Anton, Dylan was sure there was something energetic and good running in his veins. It was difficult to tell because of all the shouting and arm-waving, but it seemed to be something colourful and healthy. Something that would fill you and warm you and keep you going for a long time. Like one of those home-made, lumpy soups with bits of pasta in and maybe peas and nice crunchy bits of bacon and all sorts of things which you might fuss over on your plate but which didn't matter – in fact tasted delicious – when you'd been out in the rain with Dad all afternoon.

Dylan glanced at Lucia. Her dark skin had paled and her lips were drawn back, as if she were ready to pounce and bite. Something made him put an arm out to stop her. He moved cautiously. The man was chained by the ankles to a metal bed. A water bowl and a hunk of bread stood on a table beside him.

'Mac?' he said.

TWENTY

The man gulped and shook his great shaggy head. He definitely looked mad enough to eat worms. 'What?'

'I'm Floyd's friend,' Dylan said. 'We came to get Joe.' In theory, Mac was a grown-up, someone who could make everything alright. In practice, Dylan wasn't so sure. He became aware that Lucia was staring at him. 'This is my friend's dad,' he explained.

'*Floyd* is here? Where?' cried Mac, throwing his arms out. 'Where is everyone? They've all disappeared. So many people here and all gone. I have to find him. What day is it? I have to get to Manaus in time to tell the world how evil this project is. I have some evidence,' he smiled insanely, 'but not enough. Is it Wednesday? Unchain me – the key is there, right there.'

Dylan turned to look where he was pointing and did

indeed see a key, hanging from a hook by the window, out of Mac's reach. He looked back at Mac, who smelt a bit and who was straining at the end of his chain. Then he looked at Lucia.

'Do not unchain lunatic,' she said.

Dylan's mind raced. Miss Crassy was right, Mac was ill. But Dylan's gut told him Mac was good. Dylan had been right about Miss Crassy and Anton and he hadn't trusted his own instincts. Now his gut was telling him Mac was good, so this time, despite the fact that Mac looked crazier than anyone Dylan had ever seen, Dylan was going to go with that. He unhooked the key and crouched by Mac's left ankle to unlock it.

Lucia backed away, and bumped into a shelving unit which teetered over backwards. Dylan held his breath as it rocked forwards again and seemed to regain its balance. But the rocking had shifted all the tins to the back and the weight gave the whole unit momentum. It went crashing backwards, knocking another unit, and all its tins to the floor, too. Dylan opened the anklet and looked up at Mac, sure he had done the right thing, terrified that he had not.

'Hide,' Mac said. 'They will have heard that. They will come.'

Sure enough, at this point, shouting could be heard and the sound of men coming closer.

Mac became wild again. 'I will never escape. I will never be able to find Joe and prove...' he stopped, and crouched, backing away to the far end of the hut. The men's footsteps came closer and the door flung open. Dylan and Lucia shot behind some shelving. Anton and the two other men spread out and set off down different aisles, banging the cages and stacks of tinned food with metal poles. They would find Dylan and Lucia before they reached Mac, but the two of them squeezed together anyway, as if each one might be able to hide in the other's pockets. Through the gaps between the stacks of food, Anton's glowering face appeared and disappeared, getting larger and larger. In just a few seconds he would turn the corner.

'Excuse me.' Mac's voice boomed out from the end of the hut. He stood up and smoothed his hair down. He looked very nearly normal, but this was the most insane thing he had done yet. 'Over here,' he said, beckoning for the men to come over as if he was in a fancy restaurant, and indeed, they ran towards him, shouting and raising their metal poles.

From behind the tins, Dylan and Lucia saw them catch him, although catch wasn't really the right word for someone who was standing still with his arms on his hips, as if he had been hanging around all day for them. Anton pulled Mac's arms roughly together behind his back and tied them up.

'Time to relocate you, you noisy fool,' Anton said. 'You've brought it on yourself.' He nodded at one of the men.

Mac made a low hissing sound. He was making a theatrical effort to make Dylan look at something. At one of his bulging socks. Mac's eyes went back and forth, from Dylan's eyes down to his own right leg. Back and forth, like some joker in a pantomime. Mac went meekly with the men, until he came level with where Dylan and Lucia were hiding behind the shelves. Then he seemed to catch one foot with the other, stumbled and fell. He seemed almost to kick himself. Papers fell out of his socks. He lay on the ground for a moment, still kicking one foot against the other and, lying on the ground with his head turned towards Dylan, managed to catch Dylan's eye through the network of gaps between the tins. Under a bushy eyebrow one bulging eye winked at Dylan, full of meaning, before Mac was hauled to his feet and dragged off out of the hut.

The door banged to a close and the hut was still and quiet again.

Lucia's mouth hung open. She couldn't have looked more astonished if Pernickety had told a joke.

'Yeah, he's pretty strange, isn't he,' said Dylan. 'What?' he asked, as Lucia's expression didn't change. 'I told you Floyd said his dad was a bit mad.'

'He did that for us,' said Lucia, still gaping. 'He allowed himself captured so they not find us.'

'Oh yeah,' said Dylan. 'He's not nasty or anything. He's just ill. Fair play to Miss Crassy. She wasn't lying about that.'

'No,' cried Lucia. 'This is not madness disease. This is … trustworthy. This is first trustworthy grown-up I ever meet. Did you see? He sacrifice himself. For us. For children. Not even his children. Do you ever see grown-up do any thing for child before? Even for own children?'

'Yes,' Dylan said, thinking how Mum always chose the broken biscuits, leaving the whole ones for everyone else, and took her coat off to wrap around Tommo on the beach when it got windy. He wondered what time it was at home now and whether Tommo was sitting at the kitchen table with mum testing him on his spellings. He had hated that so much when he was at primary school, but right now he couldn't think of anything better.

'That's pretty normal, but did you hear all that about evil and saving the world? You can't take him seriously, Lucia.'

Lucia swivelled round to face him square on. Her eyes blazed and her voice came out deep and serious.

'I never in my life meet grown-up do anything for any child. My dad expel me, say I useless girl. My mum tell me I eat too much, she needs food for babies.'

'Your parents … kicked you out?'

As Dylan struggled to understand, properly understand what she had just said, it seemed as if the light had dimmed, the sun's power weakened and the planet became a different place, a shade darker than it had been. The strange thing was, she didn't sound sorry for herself. She sounded as if she was explaining what a word meant.

'This is hero man,' she said, 'to sacrifice self for useless children.'

'Oh, sure, he's a good guy,' Dylan said, pleased that she agreed with his gut instinct. 'But he is ill. What was that kicking thing he was doing on the floor? And he was winking at me like crazy.'

Lucia cautiously moved between the aisles to where Mac had stumbled on the floor. She got down on her hands and knees and looked under the pallets of tinned food. 'Aha!' she said, reaching an arm deep underneath.

She brought out Mac's phone, and held it reverentially. 'I have stolen these,' she said, 'never no one give me one.'

'Given it?'

'Yes, he was donating to us. Are you not comprehending? So we use to help him. I investigate.' She tapped on the phone. 'Oh. Password protected. Mac not ill. Those men not looking like doctors.'

'If he's not ill, why would she bring him here?'

'Mac superbly true man. I believe any item Mac say,' Lucia declared.

Dylan stared at Lucia. The rich molasses in her veins gave her certainty. They both trusted Mac, but she actually believed him, too.

For the first time Dylan considered the possibility that Mac wasn't ill, but right. Right that Miss Crassy was doing something terrible here, hidden in the Amazon rainforest. But it all looked so proper, so tidy and organised. And small.

'We have to look in the third hut,' he said. 'They must all be in there.' Whatever it was that made Mac – a clever conservationist – sound like a raving madman, that must be there too.

'So,' she said. 'We go to third hut and find Pernickety.'

'And Floyd,' Dylan said. 'And Joe.'

TWENTY-ONE

Dylan and Lucia climbed out of a back window and crouched down behind the second hut.

'What's in your tin?' Dylan asked, struggling to pull his tin out of his pocket. His stomach felt hollowed out.

'Not in this location,' Lucia said, with a horrified look on her face.

Dylan groaned.

'Don't tell me. Rule number two of the favela, never eat when you have food in your pocket and are starving hungry.'

Lucia laughed bitterly. '*When* you are starving hungry? Always starving hungry! When consuming, you not care about security. Essential find somewhere safe for eating. Sorry I discombobulate you, but possibility not here.'

'Disco-what?'

'Discombobulate. Upset. Frustrate. Confuse.'

Dylan groaned.

'I just don't want to die of hunger with two tins of hotdogs in my pocket. Gramp would say that smacks of stupidity.'

Dylan inched forwards to look down along the gap between the second and third shed. He caught a glimpse of the digger, right there in the middle of the clearing, but there was no sign of Anton, the men, or of Mac. Dylan crept under a branch with a huge waxy leaf, across to the back of the third shed and signalled to Lucia to follow. From this angle, he could see the two boats and canoe, still and calm at the small jetty. There was no sign that anyone had boarded any of them.

'It's very quiet,' he whispered, as Lucia caught up with him.

'Ominous.' She nodded.

They put their ears to the wall of the shed. Nothing. No voices, no movement. Lucia slowly rose until her eyes were just over the level of the window sill. Dylan expected her to shoot down again after one quick peep, but she kept on looking and rose higher still.

'Void,' she said at last.

'What?'

'Vacant. Empty. Is no one.' She crouched down again and her large brown eyes looked, for the first time, confused. 'They *must* be within. Nowhere else possible. Disappearing not possible.'

Dylan rose and looked in through the window. It was an office. A large desk was covered with papers and files, and diagrams were pinned up on the walls. A sofa with a stripy blue bundle on it was just visible and some chairs and mugs and a small sink and kettle were there too. As he watched, the bundle shifted.

'There is someone there – under those rugs on the sofa!' A dark head appeared, with just enough of a forehead for Dylan to be sure. 'It's Floyd! We've found Floyd!' A surge bubbled up in Dylan, up through his chest and exploded in his head. In this shed, in a clearing somewhere up the Amazon, in a country on the other side of the world, surrounded by danger, here, of all places, he felt as if he had just come home.

Dylan crept, like a baddie in a cartoon, along the side the side of shed. A small voice in his head told him that finding Floyd wasn't entirely the end of their problems, but still he wanted to shout for joy. Suddenly Floyd felt like the closest friend he had ever had.

The clearing was still empty. Boats, digger. Silence. Dylan rushed at the door and tried the handle. It was locked.

'Floyd,' he called, in something between a whisper and a cry. 'Floyd?'

There were no sounds of anyone moving inside. Lucia slipped round to the window.

'He slumbers,' she said. 'Best solution to force entry.' She joined Dylan at the door and took her bookmark out of her thesaurus. She bent it a little and slid it expertly between the thin gap between the door and the wall. When the bookmark came to the lock, she put her ear to it and wiggled it very gently. It passed slowly downwards, clicked, and the door swung open.

It was dead impressive, but Dylan didn't like to think how often she had done that. Dylan rushed past the table, knocking papers to the floor, and shook Floyd's shoulder. He couldn't wait to wake him up, to look in his eyes. He was a bit worried he might hug him. How could he have been unsure whether Floyd was a real friend or not?

'Floyd! Wake up! Floyd? Dylan moved Floyd's shoulder.

Lucia paid no interest to the sleeping bundle, but ran through the shed inspecting every corner.

'No Pernickety,' she said, before turning to the table and leafing through the papers on it.

'He won't wake up,' Dylan said.

'Much food they give him. I sleep goodly after much food,' Lucia said. She was turning the pages in a file, running her fingers down the page and reading.

'Hey, Floyd, wake up, it's me, Dylan.'

Floyd groaned and rolled slowly onto his back. He opened his eyes, saw Dylan, and groaned again.

'Go'way,' he mumbled.

'Floyd?'

'Fascinating and, moreover, enchanting,' Lucia said, standing by the medical diagrams on the wall now, walking from one to the other and slowly shaking her head. 'Picture of middle of bone, with arrows. "Spongy bone",' she read. '"Marrow".'

'Floyd! It's me. We met your dad. He's here somewhere,' Dylan said.

Floyd's eyes just managed to open. 'Daaad?' he mumbled. 'Joe?'

'We don't know where Joe is. And they've taken your dad away. How long have you been here? How did you get here?'

Floyd closed his eyes again.

'Speeeed boat…' He said. His voice was slow and low and it sounded as if it was too much effort to speak. 'Seeee Joe after fooood. Churros, mmmmm. Jam.'

'Ordinary trick,' Lucia called over her shoulder, rummaging through drawers now. 'Churros with sleeping powder in. Grown-up always use. Third rule in favela, never receive a churro. Never from anyone. Allow him sleep. He no use for some time.'

'What, so we just wait here? While he sleeps? And do nothing?'

Lucia stopped looking at papers. She checked outside the window and the door and nodded to herself.

'Now we take chance to consume our tins,' Lucia said. 'Time is grubzup.'

'About time too,' Dylan said, pulling his tin out of his

163

pocket. The label had a drawing of small brown lumps. 'Mushrooms?' he howled. 'What's in yours?'

Lucia inspected her tin.

'Cogumelos', she said. 'Mushrooms, too. Delicious.' She pulled the ring pull and scooped one from the tin and ate it.

Dylan groaned. His stomach had been nagging him for ages, but now it was screaming at him, making his head hurt, saying 'why have you done this to me? Why aren't you giving me anything to eat?' So he absolutely had to put something in it. 'Mum always said if I was hungry enough I'd like them. So here goes.' He put a mushroom in his mouth: cold, slimy, spongy yuk. He had never eaten anything so disgusting. He ate another and another. A sort of flavour was beginning to come through, something not completely disgusting. His stomach was so glad to get hold of them, and his brain was so happy to be coming back to life, that he kept on going. He reached halfway down the tin when suddenly they changed. Juicy, nutty, chewy yum. When he reached the end of the tin, he looked up at Lucia, who was flipping through papers.

'I won't tell Mum,' he said. 'It'll only encourage her.'

'Look.' Lucia held up a picture of a skeleton. 'Something else occurring here. Not only greenhouse with pretty flowers.'

It wasn't a human skeleton, because the arms were too long and the body too short, but there were similarities. The instructions were in Portuguese.

'What does it say?' Dylan asked.

'Insert needle here this angle find hip bone cavity.' Lucia looked doubtful. 'Maybe they doctor animals here, same as Mac?'

Dylan looked at the picture more closely. A large needle was pointing straight at the skeleton's hip.

'If that's true, then something really bad must be going on,' Dylan said slowly, 'just like Mac keeps saying, but where? We've looked everywhere. Nothing is wrong here. I really liked Mac, but we haven't seen anything "evil". Except Anton.'

A groan came from behind them.

'Full of … cement,' Floyd said, but his words came out more clearly than they had before.

'Hey, you've woken up!'

Floyd narrowed his eyes. 'Whaaa you doing here?'

'Whaddya think, you mush? I've come to find you. And Joe. We found Mac but he was taken away.'

Floyd glared at him. Dylan sighed. Sometimes Floyd was just too difficult. 'I thought you might be glad to see me.'

'Uh know all about yuh.' His words were slurred and Dylan had difficulty working out what he was saying. 'Uh don't need yuh anyway. Uh can do this on muh own.'

'What?' The meaning had come through, but there was no sense in what he was saying.

'Miss Crassy tol' me what yuh said. Yuh c'n stop pretending.'

'Huh? I haven't spoken to her since you went off in the limo at the airport.'

Floyd snorted. He shook his head and blinked a few times.

'Uh know she spoke to yuh on Anton's phone. Said yuh met the CEO and went home.' His eyes blazed and he muttered, 'Said yuh'd had enough of my family's mess.'

'Miss Crassy said that?' Dylan frowned. That was the nastiest thing anyone could say.

'Yeah.'

'Problematic,' Lucia said.

Dylan grabbed Floyd's arm.

'Floyd, you've got this backwards. I did meet the CEO but he told me to get lost. Miss Crassy told Anton to get rid of me. He took me to a scary part of town miles from the city centre. Dumped me there. Just chucked me out of the car. I never said anything about your family to Miss Crassy. I would never do a thing like that.'

'So Miss Crassy wa' lying? She jus' made it up?'

'YES!' Dylan yelled. 'Why would you believe her, a woman you met one day ago instead of me, who you've known for months? You're not sleepy, you're drugged. You can hardly talk. Did she take you to your dad and Joe? No!'

Floyd stared at Dylan. Or at least, he seemed to be trying to. His eyes kept swivelling away from Dylan's and back again.

'Aren't you listening?' Dylan continued. 'If it wasn't for

166

Lucia I would probably be dead by now. No one would ever know what had happened to me. I was chased by teenagers with guns and knives.'

Floyd shifted himself up onto his elbows and frowned. He spoke in slow motion, but more clearly now.

'So … if … she lied … to me … about you…'

'She could be lying about Mac being ill.'

'An' if Dad's not ill…?'

'If he's not ill, maybe he's right. Maybe it is "bloody murder", like he wrote on his wall, and evil, like he said to us just now.'

'BlueBird's evil and they're … killing?' He shook his head and slumped back on the sofa and closed his eyes.

'Maybe they're experimenting on animals. Lucia found a picture of a strangely shaped skeleton. And there are far too many cages.'

'Here?' Floyd asked, with his eyes still closed.

'No,' Dylan said, sighing. 'That's the weird thing. We've looked in the other huts and there's nothing going on.'

'Mac donated us his cellphone,' Lucia said, handing it to Floyd. 'You essential listen to Dylan. He has correctness about drugged churros. He is your friend. Your dad is hero of largest magnitude. This Crassy lady not your friend.'

Floyd pulled himself up. He frowned at Lucia.

'Who are you?' he asked, groggily, taking the phone and checking it.

'Lucia,' she answered, putting down the papers she was

looking at and holding out a hand for him to shake. 'Meaning light. Eminently useful personage, knowing many things. I come for Pernickety, you see Pernickety? Inform me. I necessary depart now.'

Floyd ignored her hand. He turned the phone on and Password flashed up.

'Where exists Pernickety?' Lucia repeated.

'Per-what?'

'My puppy.'

'Thought I dreamt it. A grey dog with crazy long legs?'

'Yes, yes, where?'

Floyd almost smiled. 'It was licking me as if I was its long lost bro...' He stopped. 'Was that a puppy?'

Lucia nodded, and picked up a wastepaper basket and tipped its contents onto the desk. 'My puppy, which I determine to retrieve from stealing men.'

'It's gonna be a rhino when it's grown, then,' Floyd murmured.

'Really, Lucia? Even the bin? Do you have to read every single piece of paper in the whole place?' Dylan asked.

'Much useful things in bin,' Lucia said. 'Just because person throw something,' here she stopped and stood a little straighter, with even more dignity, '...or someone – away, doesn't mean thing – or someone – not useful.'

'No but, seriously,' Floyd said, 'what kind of dog is ... Pernickety?'

Lucia's words about the bin had caused a strange stabbing sensation in Dylan's heart. He had no idea what to say to her, but it felt really important to say something, so he answered Floyd instead.

'I reckon she's a Great Dane,' Dylan said, looking her in the eye. 'She'll be as big this table, Lucia. She'll probably eat more than you do.'

'Hey!' Lucia held a piece of paper up in the air triumphantly. 'Inspect these diagrams. See this? Showing Amazon, creek where boats are parking, field camp, three huts. Forest all around.'

'Uh huh. So?' asked Floyd.

'Why this part of forest more verdant?'

'Lucia. Verdant?' Dylan said, crossly. There wasn't time for words like this.

'Green. Is more green. See?'

Dylan looked where her finger traced a line. The printed, coloured diagram showed the layout of the huts, surrounded by forest, which was coloured dark green. But the strange thing was that part of the dark green forest was a brighter green. A line from the field camp, leading to a round shape in the middle of the forest, was definitely brighter.

'Why would you print some of the forest a paler green?'

'Perhaps not always paler green. Perhaps was white, or blue, or red, showing track to second construction. When necessary to hide construction, you colour it green again.'

'The wrong green.'

'Then print with right green. Mistake one they throw away.'

'If they needed to hide the building from someone,' Floyd said.

'Exactly,' Dylan said.

All three of them looked at each other.

'If Mac is right, this must be where it's happening.'

'That's what Joe said in his last email.' Floyd was sitting bolt upright now. 'That Dad kept going on about a second project and how he was going to expose it. And what's this?' Floyd asked, pointing to an X on the printout.

Lucia translated. 'Emergency exit,' she said. 'Near bank of side river.'

'Perhaps we could go in that way?' Dylan suggested. It would mean trailing through the rainforest until they hit the river, then following it all the way around and hoping there was some sort of obvious place to turn off. With no real map, just a simple diagram.

'Don't be daft,' Floyd said. 'It's right in the forest and we definitely don't want to go in there.' He put his finger on the round patch of green. 'Joe must be there, then,' he said, in a soft voice.

'Pernickety similarly … inhabits such a location,' Lucia said, with exactly the same softness.

'And Mac and Anton and Miss Crassy,' Dylan said impatiently. 'And this thin line comes to here, look,' he pointed to the diagram. 'Which I reckon is where that boarding is. I bet there isn't any fence behind it. If everything Mac has said is true, he needs help. And it has to be fast, because Miss Crassy has to be back in Manaus for tomorrow afternoon. If she becomes Global Head of Special Projects, she'll be even more powerful than she already is. Whatever she's doing here, she'll have the power to do all over the world. So we have to go. Right now.'

'But … what can we do when we get there?' Floyd asked. 'We can't fight them, we can't rescue Joe and Dad from Anton and his men, can we? We aren't superheroes.'

'Mac donated phone,' Lucia said. 'Why? Must be a reason. To use as camera? Maybe so we send evidence of malevolent doings.'

'Exactly!' Dylan said, standing up. 'We can take photos of what's happening. Remember those scrunched-up letters in your dad's flat? They all said that if he had evidence of what was going on, they wanted to know. That's the only thing he hasn't managed to do. And it's the only thing we can do. We get to this … round place, take photos, get out again.'

'And liberate Pernickety.'

'And get Joe and Dad.'

Dylan sighed. Didn't they get it? It was wildly ambitious to hope they could get photos without being caught, never mind get out again, or work out how to send the photos to people who could do something about it. But at least it was a plan. 'Sure,' he said, 'and we'll save the world while we're at it. Let's go. We've got to get there and back before it gets dark.'

Floyd stretched, shook his head and groaned. 'I still feel like I'm under water,' he said.

'Come on,' Dylan said, heaving him to his feet. 'We've come five thousand, five hundred and sixty-eight miles. One more won't kill you.' Though something in the pit of his stomach told him it just might.

TWENTY-TWO

The boarding pulled away to reveal a rough track through the trees, lined by low fences on either side. It curved around to the left in a wide semi-circle. They were just about to go through it when Lucia stopped them.

'Wait,' she said, with a thoughtful look. She turned round to stare at the boats moored in the creek. 'That one,' she muttered, and ran off to the motor boat, jumping on board. She scrabbled around and came back dangling a key triumphantly.

'Pernickety and me have home now! And transport. Ha ha!'

'You're gonna steal a boat?' Floyd asked.

'Yup, that's exactly what she's doing,' Dylan said. 'Come on.'

Floyd just managed to walk, with his arms over Dylan's and Lucia's shoulders, and they set off along the track.

They soon realised their mistake. Male voices came towards them from around the bend, arguing in Portuguese.

Dylan, Floyd and Lucia stared at each other.

'Over the fence,' Dylan hissed.

Lucia scrambled over, but Floyd stood stock still.

'Floyd! Quick! Come on!'

Floyd reached the fence, but seemed unable to climb over. Dylan grabbed one arm, and the waist of his trousers.

'Help me, Lucia, pull him over!'

Floyd fell over the fence and Dylan followed him just as the men came into view, shouting at each other. Dylan dragged Floyd back in among the trees. From their hiding place they watched the men approaching. One man shoved the other and got a bang on the ear back. More shouting.

'What are they saying?' Dylan whispered as the men came closer.

'Both astonish at stupidity of other. Both assign blame to other. One of them brought wrong needles from field camp, but definitely was other's fault. Both very scared Miss Crassy achieve fury.'

The men disappeared down the track, still arguing.

'We can't risk going back onto the track again,' Dylan said. 'We'll have to find a way to the emergency entrance.'

And he took a good look around, into the depths of the Amazonian rainforest.

A few slanting shafts of sunlight glanced through the crowded treetop canopy, but they weren't strong enough to brighten the heavy shade. With each footstep, smells wafted up, of something like tea-leaves, or rain or the herby stuff Mum put in stews. A brief knocking drum roll made Dylan look to his left, where a creamy woodpecker with a tufted red head and a long sharp beak battered away at a trunk.

Dylan bent beneath a branch, climbed over a fallen log and nearly tripped over a swooping root which slid upwards until it joined the biggest tree trunk he had ever seen. He gazed up and up. The tree was so high that Dylan had to bend his head as far back as it would go, to gaze at a fuzzy mess of bright greenery, spangled by sunlight.

Dylan couldn't see any creatures, but he could sense them everywhere. A strange orchestra was tuning up, with layers of noise overlapping each other. The high whine of mosquitos was punctuated by crickets buzzing. Something flew overhead, the branches waved, and 'choo-choo-choo, piroo-piroo' sounded from a flock of small birds. Something scampered by their feet, and the ground rustled and shifted. Something crept away at a distance and nothing but tiny fragments of shadows moved.

'This whole place is alive!' Above Floyd's shoulder, on a

thin, pale green stem, was a bright blue frog with black markings, blue as blue could be, and still a bit bluer than that. It had to be plastic.

'Hey, look,' he said, and reached out to pick it up.

'Beware danger!' Lucia cried, pulling his arm back. 'This specimen a poison dart frog. Exist in many different colours. Entire planet not contain more poisonous animal anywherever. One frog contain enough poison to kill ten men. Some so poisonous they murder you simply by touch.'

'Wow!'

'Necessary also to tuck trousers into socks. You no desire anywhichever to scramble up leggings. Bare feet safer.'

'What sort of thing?' Dylan asked, tucking a trouser leg in.

'Snakes, leeches, biting ants. Evidently existing many hundred species in rainforest that best not to endure up leg. Perhaps now not superb time for comprehensive list.'

'How do you know all this?' asked Floyd, bending down.

Lucia shrugged.

'Once I find document in rubbish tip. Holiday insurance in the Amazon. You astonish at how many problematics here. If you swimming with cut on leg, piranha fish will transform nice fat leg to sorry clean bone.'

'My mum says there's a place in London where you can

get tiny fish to eat all the dead skin off your feet,' Floyd said. 'A friend of hers did it. You sit with your feet in a footbath. It tickles, she said.'

'That is disgusting,' Dylan and Lucia said, at the same time. Dylan saw the look on Lucia's face and knew his face looked exactly the same. It made him laugh, but his laughter came out too fast and the panic he was feeling began to bubble up. If he didn't stop laughing right now, he might have to sit down and cry.

'Come on,' he said, sternly. 'We've got to get there before it gets dark.'

'Hey, wait,' Floyd said, looking back at the way they had come. 'Already we can't see the track. The rainforest has closed up behind us.' His voice trembled.

Dylan turned back. Floyd was right.

'Wait. Necessary to understand phone for photography and recording before advancing. Floyd, you educate me.'

'Sure,' Floyd said, pulling Mac's phone out of his pocket. 'But the first thing you must learn is to conserve the battery. Turn it off whenever you're not using it and keep the light really dim. We won't be able to charge it so we have to be really careful.'

He looked down at the phone and gasped.

'It's got signal! That is mad. There must be something big going on somewhere. Trouble is, I need to guess his password.' He tapped something in. HoFloJo. 'No,' he said. He tried again. HoFloJo3. 'No,' he shook his head. 'I know!' he said, and tapped hOflOjO3.

The phone sprang to life with a photo of a log and strange orange and brown stripey fungus ballooning out all over it.

'How did you guess that?' Dylan asked. 'That's a tricky password.'

'I should have known he wouldn't put the capitals in the right place. He's too clever for that. hO is short for Hope, my mum, flO is short for Floyd and…'

'Ok, I get it. But three?'

'He always called us his favourite three.'

'I bet he thought it was a really good password, too.'

'He did, actually. I remember when he got the phone telling me I'd never guess it. So I've spent quite a lot of time thinking about it.'

Floyd flipped to the contact list and found exactly seven contacts: the World Wildlife Organisation, the CEO of BlueBird, the *National Geographic*, the BBC news, CNN, *The Guardian* and the *Cambrian Weekly*. No friends, no family. He opened the photos and found shots of empty cages, shots of the fieldcamp and several pictures of dense greenery. 'Hmm. Nothing much.'

Lucia asked Floyd to show her how you could send emails. She seemed to understand everything the first time he explained it, and asked more and more questions: about how to take a photo, how to use the video, how to find stuff out, how to tell if the signal was weak or strong.

Dylan couldn't concentrate. There were only a few hours of daylight left and they had no idea how to get to the round place. Floyd didn't seem to understand the danger they were in, but then Floyd, he realised, hadn't actually been scared yet. He had fallen asleep trusting Miss Crassy and woken to find Dylan there. Dylan had a feeling Lucia would survive absolutely anything, so it was up to Dylan to keep them on track, find the way to the round place, get Joe and Mac – and Pernickety – and get out of again.

If he could find a tall enough tree that was easy to climb, he might be able to see the way. That's what he told himself, anyway. If he had had to be a little more honest, if Matt had been there and asked him exactly what he thought he was doing, climbing a tree at this exact moment, he might have admitted that if he didn't get away from them, get up high, alone, he might just lose it, and fear would pour out of him.

Just a few feet away there was a narrow tree with creepers wound around it, forming sloping steps you could probably climb on. It wasn't tall enough though. He came to a palm tree with giant vicious thorns sticking out of it in circles all the way up, and another tree with long horizontal branches that would be just right for lying on.

He turned round. He had gone too far. He couldn't see Floyd and Lucia. He retraced his steps, passing the spikey palm tree, then saw another spikey palm tree and another. He couldn't be sure which way to go. It all looked the same. He nearly called out, then stopped himself.

He found a taller tree with the same strong creepers

winding around it. He put a hand out to feel the bristly trunk of the creeper in his palm. He ran his hand along the curled form, feeling the roughness. Maybe no other human being in the history of the world would ever touch this particular creeper, or ever see it curling in exactly this way. He began to feel calmer. Maybe no one else would ever walk right here, and see this secret tangle of life and death. He pulled on the creeper and it didn't break away. He started climbing, and climbed up and up, easily treading on its thick, curving stems, Tarzan-like. It gave him the same feeling as stomping to the top of the hill at home, getting up high, away from everything. Even if you didn't know how to sort things out, at least you were busy and soon there would be nothing but big sky above you, space to think. A brightly coloured bird squawked and flew up, and as it turned he saw a toucan's enormous orange and green beak and the blue patch around its eye.

He climbed higher still, drawn up towards the light. It was so easy, with branches and the creeper providing handholds and footholds. The further up he went, and the more birds that fluttered or swooped or glided past, the calmer he felt. When the tree trunk was thin enough to put his arm around it and hold on, he stopped to gaze out in all directions. His tree wasn't higher than all the other trees, but the canopy was thinner up here and he could see through it a fair way. There was no round building.

A soft rain began to fall, landing lightly on his hair and shoulders. The clouds moved slowly, and reminded

Dylan of the poster of the water cycle in the geography classroom at school. Where had this rain come from? Maybe some of these drops had evaporated from his river last summer, blown over the Atlantic, all five thousand, five hundred and sixty-eight miles of it, like he had, and landed here, on him. He stuck his tongue out and caught a soft drop. Maybe that drop came from his river, was one of the very drops he had seen leaping up between his feet as he sat on the tree trunk. He took some deep breaths and admitted it to himself. He was as daft as a brush and he had no idea how they would get through the rainforest to the round building. He had absolutely no plan at all.

A branch to his left moved. It reached vertically up to another branch, grew a claw and pulled itself up. It grew a head, a face, eyes and a mouth. There, hanging from one long arm, exactly the same mottled brown and white as the tree trunk, was a furry creature with big soppy eyes, a funny haircut and an unmistakeable smile. A sloth.

Dylan's heart battered about. He was just a few feet away from one of the gentlest creatures on the planet. With its other arm, the animal pulled a twig from the tree and slowly, as slowly as Tommo licked a mint choc-chip ice-cream on a hot day at Aberdovey, ate each leaf. When it had finished, it dropped the bare twig and, still smiling, curled, very, very slowly and comfortably, up into a ball in the fork of the tree. Dylan watched it until he was sure it had gone to sleep, his fear slipping away with every moment.

He might not have a plan yet, but the sloth, like the butterflies, had at least taken away his panic. He didn't know exactly what he was going to do, but he would keep on trying. Tommo would love this story. He would ask for it again and again and Dylan would remember every single detail to tell him.

He had to show Floyd and Lucia the sloth. He scrambled down, dangling from one arm, taking risks, bouncing down from branch to branch, to get the real monkey feel. He was at the last branch, about to drop to the ground when he saw him. A boy, whacking the trunk of an enormous grey tree with a thick branch.

TWENTY-THREE

It wasn't an ordinary tree trunk. Not round, but with folds around it, a bit like a skirt. Three or four pleats swooped up out of the ground, narrowing as they reached the trunk, as if the tree needed more support than a round trunk could give. But the boy was ordinary. He wore blue shorts, flip flops and a red and yellow football T-shirt – the Ghanain strip – Dylan recognised it from the World Cup – with a 9 on it.

Each time the boy hit the tree, a loud, deep echoing hum rang out over all the other sounds. The last boy Dylan had seen whacking a tree trunk was Floyd, last summer, and Dylan had been completely wrong about why he was doing it. So this time Dylan watched. The boy lifted the huge branch, swung it away, then hit a narrow wooden pleat as hard as he could. He was red in the face, just as Floyd had been. He did it three times, waited, did it three more times. Then he dropped the stick and bent down to pick something up.

'Hey!' Dylan called.

The boy turned round easily, a smile on his face. When he saw Dylan, his eyes widened. 'Ola,' he said.

Dylan half wanted to know why he was hitting the tree and half wanted to get the boy to take them to the round building, right now.

'Are you lost?'

'Ar oo ost?' the boy said, laughing, his veins fizzing with life.

'Hey, Lucia, Floyd, come here!' Dylan called, and after a while, and some crashing about, they appeared, from such an unexpected direction that Dylan briefly realised just how lost he had been.

Lucia spoke to the boy in Portuguese and he frowned. She spoke again, more slowly. His face cleared and he answered, waving his arms, pointing off into the forest and then down at the plastic bag at his feet.

'Boy is collecting brazil nuts,' she said, 'and whacking of tree informs his mother in village he's OK and passing night in forest.'

The boy said something and pointed to his chest, grinning.

'His name is Tochi,' Lucia said. She asked him something and he shrugged. 'But he says no one remembers what it means.'

'Ask him about the place we're looking for,' Dylan said. 'Don't tell him anything about it, just ask if he can take us there?'

When Lucia did this, the boy's face clouded over. Picking up his bag of nuts he turned away, saying something to himself. His muttering grew louder as he walked away, shaking his head.

'Wait! Tell him he can't leave us here. What's the matter?'

Lucia translated. 'He say if we belong to that place the jaguars can chew on us all night and he will be glad. He say is evil. Kills the sloths.'

'That's what I wanted to tell you! I saw a sloth!' Dylan said. 'It's just up there. Tell him.' He pointed up to where he remembered it, but could see nothing but mottled brown branches.

Lucia told Tochi this, who started yelling. He went on and on, and Lucia's face became more and more serious.

'He says once were many sloths, you see four or five each morning, lots with their babies. The round building people are spoiling everything.'

'Lucia, you have to tell him there's a woman there who will have power to build more secret places and kill more sloths if we can't stop her. Tell him Floyd has lost his brother and we think he is there. Say we are the only people who can do something about this and we need to get there right now, before it gets dark. And tell him he is the only person in the whole world who can help us.'

When Tochi heard this, he pointed at himself.

'Mim?' he said.

'Me?' translated Lucia.

Dylan and Floyd nodded. Then Tochi stared at Floyd and said two words.

'Your brother?' Lucia translated, and Floyd nodded. Tochi went over to Floyd and put a hand on his shoulder. Tochi then looked at Dylan and spoke.

'He inform he will guide us there but not enter because he frightening of evil spirits. And anyway too late today. He guide us early-early tomorrow.'

'No! Tell him tomorrow is too late. Miss Crassy will be leaving tomorrow and we have to get there before then.'

Lucia told Tochi, but, since he just frowned, tried explaining it a different way. She turned to Dylan. 'Tochi not listening hardly in Portuguese lessons, I am thinking,' she said disapprovingly. Eventually she came back with his answer.

'He says sun will descend before we are arriving there.'

'How does he know? It's not getting dark yet.'

'How are you not knowing? Sun appearing at six in morning, setting at six in evening. Every day.'

'OK, fine. We'll go in at night. We'll have a better chance if half of them are asleep. But we have to go right now, Lucia. Tell him. We can't wait until tomorrow.'

Lucia relayed all this, and came back with the answer.

'Not possible tonight. We will be meeting jaguars and providing them dinner. Only can reach night hut and make food. Speediest way is by river. Through middle of forest. He can transport us in boat.'

Tochi stood with his arms crossed and his face set. You could see that nothing was going to change his mind.

'Looks like we don't have a choice,' Dylan said, with what felt like the last breath in his body. And as soon as he accepted this fact, and completely gave in to it, he was overwhelmed with a feeling of exhaustion.

Ever since the moment when he saw the apple core roll towards the drain and decided to try to find Floyd, he had been making progress. Finding Mac, avoiding Anton and his men, persuading Floyd of the truth – all these things had got him closer to finding Joe and getting home again. But now he had hit a brick wall – Tochi – and he realised how bone tired he was, and how difficult it had all been.

'Fine,' he said wearily. 'Early-early tomorrow then.'

The boat turned out to be a canoe, which was moored on a narrow waterway between trees. When they were all settled into it, it was so low in the water that the tiniest tilt left or right let water in. Dylan sat very still as Tochi kneeled up front, steering the canoe with a paddle. They moved silently through the water, coming into a small lake.

'A red daddy long legs has just crawled out of the bottom of my trousers,' Dylan said.

'I suppose,' Floyd said slowly, 'that's a good thing.'

Dylan trailed his hand in the water. There was nothing

he could do but sit in this incredibly slow canoe, gliding over the water. Somehow it didn't stop him from feeling as if he was just about to sprint a hundred metres.

Tochi turned and saw Dylan's fingers in the water. He shrieked something, gabbling and signalling for Dylan to pull his hand back.

'He say caiman everywhere. Amazonian crocodiles,' Lucia said. 'Not clever to donate hand.'

Tochi held up one hand, signalling for them to listen while he made a series of deep sounds in the back of his throat, grunting audibly. From all around them under the water came quiet answering grunts.

'The caiman heard him? And they answered? Ask him if they eat people,' Dylan said.

Lucia translated and Tochi burst out laughing and answered her.

'He says no, they don't like the taste, so they'll spit you out.'

'Oh,' Dylan said.

'Are there piranha?' Floyd asked.

'Many,' came the answer. In the bottom of the canoe was a bag with a few purple berries in, and a long stick with a nylon thread hanging from it and a simple metal hook at the end. Tochi pulled the paddle in and attached one of the purple berries to the end of the hook. He gave the fishing rod to Floyd and mimed how to keep it joggling up and down in the water. After a while, Floyd pulled a small grey fish out of the water.

'Piranha!' he yelled.

But Tochi shook his head. He paddled to a small inlet and, taking the fish from Floyd, used its flesh for bait. He swung the bait up in the air and smacked it on the water, letting it drift down a few centimetres deep before repeating the action. Dylan sat in silence, feeling the seconds tick by, wondering if Miss Crassy had left yet, then trying to distract himself by watching the rod, willing it to be jerked down.

'What are those trees, with huge red baubles on?' Floyd asked. 'And white mop heads? They look like something out of Dr Seuss. Like truffula trees or something.'

Lucia asked, and Tochi said, 'Munguba,' and then began to get angry again.

'He say white fruit of munguba tree favourite food for sloths. Should be sloth in that tree. White fruit should be all gone.'

The fishing rod jerked and Tochi pulled it up. A round fish, about the size of a fist with an orange belly, flapped at the end. He held the fish carefully and unhooked it, dropping it into the boat, where it jumped and flapped and snapped its sharp white teeth. Dylan slid a leaf into its mouth and held it there while it snapped shut. When the fish opened its mouth again, Dylan pulled the leaf away. It had a semicircle missing and neat tooth marks all around the gap.

'Wow,' he said.

When seven piranha lay in the boat, Tochi paddled

across the loop in the river to the reeds on the other side of the creek. He leapt out first and pulled the canoe further up and onto the bank. He took them to a simple wooden shelter built in a tree, with palm leaves as a floor covering. The sky was turning pale blue and pink and orange and the clouds were darkening from white to a solid grey.

'He says we have to be quick, finding wood for a fire before sun goes down,' Lucia said, so they all ran around gathering twigs and logs and kindling for Tochi to build into a small pyramid.

'I bet he's got a brilliant way of lighting a fire,' Dylan whispered to Floyd. 'I bet he'll rub two sticks together and it'll just burst into flame.'

Tochi took a lighter out of his shorts pocket and lit the pyramid from the inside. The tiny twigs caught and spread until a good blaze fired up. When it had died down and left a hot glowing base, he cut up the piranha and arranged them over the embers. He took a bottle of golden liquid out of his bag to share and when the first gulp went down Dylan's throat, he thought he was drinking pure gold. For five solid seconds, as he drank, he wasn't panicking about Miss Crassy and Joe and Mac. All he was thinking about was how much he liked Tochi and what fun they would have if they had more time.

'That's amazing,' he said, wiping his mouth with the back of his hand. This must be what ran in Tochi's veins.

'Guarana!' Tochi said, making a thumbs-up sign and grinning.

'Similar to cola,' Lucia said. 'But my like guarana better.'

They sat and ate fish and brazil nuts and drank guarana as the treetops turned black and the sun slithered away in purple and lilac streaks. Before it had completely gone, and still glinted on the surface of the water just a few metres away from them, three large bright pink forms broke the water right by the edge of the tributary, like hills that appeared and sank again.

'What on earth were they?' Dylan asked, swallowing the last of his share of the drink.

'Botos,' Tochi said.

'Dolphins,' Lucia said. 'Pink river dolphins, called botos. Look, they appear again!'

As Dylan watched their black eyes and pink backs rise up and curl away, he shook his head.

'Everything in this country is the wrong colour,' he said. 'Purple potatoes, blue frogs, brown and yellow stripy rivers, red daddy long legs and now pink dolphins. This is a crazy, crazy country.' Gramp had been completely wrong. Things were not the same all over the world at all.

They all laughed, except for Floyd who didn't even smile. Dylan knew it had nothing to do with the drugged churros now. His veins were solid ice again. He was going to be no good at all in getting anything done.

In the night shelter were two hammocks, so they lay two in each, top to toe, under rough blankets. With Floyd's feet right by his shoulder, Dylan listened to the winding down of the orchestra, the croaking and humming of frogs, the last piroo-piroos, a soft, sad foghorn sound and a few solitary peeps, like a referee's whistle. It was completely black and almost quiet. Mosquito bites itched all round Dylan's ankles and wrists but they were nothing compared to the worries popping up inside him: about what would happen in the morning, whether they would get there before Miss Crassy left, whether Mac was OK. But the last thought was the worst because he knew Floyd hadn't faced it yet: was Joe still alive?

Dylan counted six hours onwards. Midnight. Everyone at home would be asleep. Tommo with his cars parked by his pillow, Gramp snoring, possibly sleeping in the same vest and pants he had worn during the day. None of them would be worried about who was still alive, or even about how to get home. Only owls and bats would be awake, searching for fieldmice and insects. Matt and Aled and Rob would be sleeping like babies, in rows. And to think Rob had been afraid of going to Harlech.

He couldn't sleep because a question lurked at the back of his mind. It had been there ever since Mustafa Shadid had told him there was a bigger picture. Was he wrong to care about his farm and his life? Was it stupid to fight against things? All his life he had fought against school, worked to make dens and tracks, tried his best to help Dad with ideas for the farm. Was all that wrong? Were you supposed to just do what everyone expected you to do? Were you supposed to be a robot? From where he was, deep in the rainforest, covered in mosquito bites, miles and miles away from everyone except a few ruthless adults, fighting things didn't seem the best strategy in the world. He tried to think of what might happen the next day so he could make a plan, but since the last two days had been completely beyond anything he could have imagined, his mind went blank. What if they found that Joe, Mac and Pernickety were all dead? What would they do then? Turn round and come home? A huge hopeless sigh left his chest. He was safe here, in this treehouse, for the next few hours. After that anything could happen.

Then he had a thought. Treehouse? So one of his plans *had* worked. Here he was, lying in a hammock with a bunch of friends in a treehouse at half-term. Just in the wrong tree, in the wrong forest, in the wrong country, on the wrong continent. If he ever got out of here, ever got home, if this was ever over, he must remember to find that funny.

TWENTY-FOUR

The sky was still black when he woke from a nightmare about an enormous roaring monster, big enough to eat the whole night shelter in one mouthful. He blinked, fully awake. The terrifying sound boomed out again. It wasn't a dream. He sat up and fell out of the hammock onto the wooden floor. The huge toothy jaws of a T-Rex were nowhere to be seen, but he was definitely awake and the noise of animal fury was everywhere, all around him, in his chest, high above his head, filling his mind with claws and saliva and greedy eyes.

'Tochi?' Dylan whispered urgently, and heard him mumble something to Lucia. The roaring was everywhere.

'Howler monkeys,' she said. 'He says they discover good fruity breakfast and don't want anywhichever animal to steal it.'

'Monkeys can make that much noise? They can sound that scary?' His shoulders melted back into their normal place.

'Probably only six of them, he say.'

Pale blue showed above the trees and over there, in silhouette, three monkeys scampered on all fours along a branch and out of sight. It was thrilling, being right in the middle of the Amazonian rainforest listening to howler monkeys roaring like a monster in a bad horror movie because they had found a good fruit salad. But this was Thursday morning, the day Miss Crassy would compete for Global Head of Special Projects.

'We have to get up, we have to go now,' he said, his voice sounding ridiculously small and weak. Back home, as long as he was outside, he always felt strong. Now he wasn't sure he would ever feel strong again.

Tochi led them all away from the night shelter, apparently in a random direction. They walked in silence as the sky grew light. Without warning, Tochi stopped and they all bumped into each other.

'He says he not step further.'

'But where is it?' Dylan asked. It wasn't as if they had arrived anywhere. He glanced around to see if he had missed something. And then he got it. Over in the distance the mad tangle seemed to be all tidied up. It was still made up of branches and greenery but creepers grew in straight lines, rather than curvily. Dylan looked more carefully. The colours were wrong, too – a branch was the same

195

brown all over, the greens were all the same green. And they were all flat, as if they'd been painted on something, with nothing protruding, nothing sticking out. Dylan blinked and shook his head. It was boarding, painted to look like the rainforest. If you just glanced at it, you wouldn't notice.

Dylan led the others towards it, picking his way over over a trail of leaf-cutter ants on a march home.

He came to a massive painted wall.

He smoothed his hand over the surface and felt something sticking out.

'It's got a handle. It's a door. This is it. We're going in.' Dylan's stomach heaved itself over in one heavy roll. He turned back to look at the others. Tochi was standing at a distance, smiling encouragingly.

'Goodbye, Tochi,' Dylan said. 'Thank you.'

Dylan twisted the handle and pushed. It opened onto blackness.

TWENTY-FIVE

Dylan stepped inside. Three steps later, he could see nothing. The warm stickiness of the jungle morning had been cut away and cold made his skin shrink into his bones. An odd smell of wet pavement enveloped him. What he was standing on was solid, but it wasn't flat. It seemed to curl up at the sides. Dylan put his hand out and felt the clammy wall curl over his head.

'It's a concrete pipe,' Floyd said and his words echoed, 'pipe, pipe, pipe' getting less clear and more eerie as the sound disintegrated into a hum and then into nothing.

'It might go on for ever,' Dylan said, blinking.

'Luminoso!' called Lucia.

'Has she read Harry Potter?' Floyd asked. 'Does she think...'

'Luminoso! Brightness!' she said.

Sure enough, if Dylan blinked hard, a pale glimmer could be seen in the distance. His heart began to thump in his ears. That must be half a mile away, deep in the Amazonian rainforest. The blackness swam before his eyes, the pale glimmer dancing about ahead.

'Can this be right?' Floyd asked.

Dylan's breath came faster. Never in his life had he been so far away from fresh air and a view of the sky. He began to run towards the spot of light, willing it to get larger. As it grew, there came a strange sound, a bit like rushing water. The closer they got, the more it sounded like barking. But not the barking of one or two, or even six dogs. It was more like the high-pitched barking of dozens of puppies.

The light became a glow. Dylan could see his own feet, and when he turned to look back, the features on Lucia's face. She didn't look at all scared, just determined. Behind her, Floyd's face was also set.

At last they came to wide strips of thick plastic sheeting which formed a barrier between the end of the huge concrete pipe and the terrible brightness that seemed to come from behind it.

'Daylight is much brighter than I remembered,' mumbled Dylan, pushing through the plastic sheeting. He turned to look at the others. Emergency exit, it said, over the top of the tunnel they had just come out of.

It wasn't daylight. A white domed ceiling stretched out above them, supported by a complicated skeleton of poles, like an enormous polytunnel. Through its pale plasticky membrane you could see the shadows of branches and trees outside it, and even the silhouette of a bird, flying above.

Rows and rows of shelving and aisles shot off into the distance, towards the centre of the domed construction, like some sort of nightmarish white supermarket. It seemed there was a space in the centre, with tables and chairs and computers on, all in white. Technicians in white coats moved slowly in and out of sight. Beyond the central space were more aisles and shelves, stretching out towards the far end of the dome, all with nothing but cages.

Lucia spoke in Dylan's right ear.

'Such a cacophony,' she said.

'Cacophony. Right.'

Floyd moved forwards and spoke into Dylan's left ear.

'What a racket,' he said.

Dylan, Lucia and Floyd crept forwards along the closest aisle and peered into the first cage.

A puppy was jumping up and down against the cage door, yelping croakily as if its voice was about to give out. Dylan put his hand up to the bars and felt its tiny warm tongue desperately licking the palm of his hand. If he closed his eyes for one second and ignored the noise, he could pretend he was at home in the kitchen with Megs. In the next cage, the puppy was lying down but Dylan could just hear its high whine among all the noise. Every cage held a puppy, either jumping up and crashing against its bars, or lying down, whining. From where he stood, Dylan could see into several cages: there was a shaggy white puppy, here a short-haired brown one, a spotty one, a brindled one. And there was one just like Megs, with the same black and white markings, her big eyes showing the whites, and anger bolted through him. They were all different, except for one thing. Each one was skinny and you could see their ribs and the shadows between each rib. Even worse than the sight of so many desperate caged puppies, was the smell. It had the sharp, dirty smell of fear.

Lucia was darting from cage to cage, taking photos with Mac's phone and mouthing, 'Pernickety? Pernickety?' when all of a sudden there was a loud crackle, like electronic lightning, and every puppy yelped at the same time and then collapsed on the floor of their cage in silence.

From somewhere deep among the aisles, perhaps in the central space, came a furious roar.

'You vile monster!' An English voice with a strong Welsh accent.

'Dad!' yelled Floyd, then clapped a hand over his mouth.

A cry went up and footsteps came running towards them. Lucia shot off back up the aisle and off to one side. Floyd and Dylan stopped dead, half-hoping it was Mac coming towards them.

It was too late to hide. Men and women in white coats,

holding test tubes, or carrying puppies, rushed towards them, shouting.

Dylan couldn't understand any of the words, but their meaning was clear. He had never seen such angry adults in real life. Strong arms grabbed Dylan and hauled him and Floyd towards the central space, to the white cabinets and sinks and taps and huge jars of what looked like a thick grey paste. It was the sort of apparatus they had in the chemistry lab at school. This enormous structure was a laboratory. An animal whose body was as big as Pernickety's, but furrier, clawed and long-limbed lay on a table, asleep or dead, and a woman held a huge needle over its hip. She looked cross, as if all the commotion was distracting her. Dylan caught a glimpse of the sloth's face, and saw it had the same sweet smile as the one in the forest.

Anton, still in his grey suit, glowered over Mac, who was tied, slumped, to a chair. One arm was tied behind his back and the other hung down all wrong, twisted round so that the palm faced backwards, as if it had been only half-screwed on at the elbow. His camera still hung from his neck, which was purple with bruises.

'Stupido!' yelled Anton.

'Dad!' called Floyd again, his voice breaking slightly. Mac's head turned slowly round and Dylan was shocked to see how different he looked from their first meeting just the day before. His face was colourless, his mouth half open in a concrete smile.

'Floyd, my lad!' he managed to say. 'Stupendous to see you! Your friends said you were around.'

'Dad?' Floyd sounded stunned.

'Things have got a bit tricky, my boy. Ah – I'll think of something shortly. These creatures,' he nodded towards Anton, 'won't be troubling us much longer I shouldn't think. And, uh, I've got it all worked out. When this is over, I'm coming back to work near you and Mum. I found a farm that's perfect for a BlueBird project – right in your village – I'll be working there.'

'Oh, Dad!'

Dylan's head grew light and airy as if it was a huge space with only one idea floating around in it. A Bluebird project? In their village? That Mac had found? So it was all Mac's fault. That was why Dad's farm had been bought by BlueBird. All Mum's questions – Why our farm? – had just been answered. It was because one of Mac's jobs had been to find a farm to grow moss on, and he wanted to work near his family. Dylan opened his mouth, but only a strange sound came out.

Floyd whipped round and gazed at Dylan with an agonised look.

'You!' Anton cried, gawping at Dylan and taking a step backwards. For a split second Anton looked almost frightened. Then he recovered himself and yelled something in Portuguese.

As Dylan was hauled towards a chair and his arms were yanked behind him, he caught sight of Lucia, darting between the aisles, taking photos on Mac's phone. He felt the rough texture of rope scraping against his wrists and saw that Floyd was also being tied up.

While Anton and the others were busy with the ropes and yelling at Mac and each other, Lucia came terrifyingly close. She took photos of the equipment on the central table, of the test tubes and the labels on them, and of the white-coated technicians from different angles. Dylan didn't dare watch her in case they turned to see what he was looking at, but they were all busy shouting and tying them up or trying to hold Mac still, at the same time as avoiding his feeble kicks. Lucia caught Dylan's eye and shook her head and went on taking photos.

Everyone fell silent as quick clipped footsteps came marching towards them from the far end of the laboratory. The technicians drew together into a tight group.

Miss Crassy appeared, keys dangling from her waist. Her long blonde hair lay perfectly straight behind her back. In one hand she held some documents and in the other, a small glass bottle filled with something grey.

'What's all this fuss and cussing about? It's as hot as blazes out there, I need to leave for my presentation and…'

Her eyes nearly popped out of her head when she saw Dylan.

'You again! Jeez Louise. Anton! Why is eco-kid still

breathing? Is the Amazon not big enough to lose one boy in? Did you need a bigger river, hey?'

Her eyes blazed as she went up to Mac and unlooped the camera from around his neck. Without saying anything, but with a small smile, Miss Crassy took the memory stick out and threw it to the stone floor. Then she put her orange heel on it and crunched it. It was definitely not just purple water running in her veins. She spoke quietly in Portuguese to one of the technicians. She seemed to be asking whether Dylan and Floyd had seen the far end of the laboratory, past the central tables. The technician shook his head, and Miss Crassy's face softened very slightly.

'You have put me in a darn difficult position,' she sighed, turning to Mac and Dylan and Floyd. 'One day, when the world enjoys the fruits of our labours, they will be glad of our work and questions won't be asked. If you had any cow sense, Mac, you'd have just looked the other way.' She stuck her chin in the air and blinked.

There was something else, Dylan thought. Mac had been right about the animals, but there was something worse.

'Anyway. It's too late for that now.' She turned to Anton. 'We'll have to chuck them all out together.' She slowly tucked her hair away behind her ears, showing a perfectly tanned forehead. She looked absolutely beautiful. 'Do I got to spell it out, Anton? You're gonna tie their hands behind their backs,' she paused to let the instruction sink in, 'put them in sacking,' another pause, 'and then you're gonna dump them in the river,' she drawled. 'Is that, like, clear enough for you? Have I left anything out? So busy up, I'm in a hurry!'

Anton avoided Dylan's eyes, but he came so close that Dylan could smell the rank tang of sour cream. Anton threw a sack over Dylan's head, and Dylan felt his arms being untied from the chair. A blow knocked him onto the floor and Dylan rolled over onto his face as Anton fiddled with the mouth of the sack, tying it up, he guessed. Then things went still. Dylan wriggled around, got himself into a sitting position. His breathing was coming too fast and he was losing control. He mustn't lose control. If he panicked and started yelling they would get rid of him even quicker.

Through the tiny holes in the sacking he could see figures moving but no faces. A terrible thought blew a hole in his stomach. He might never see another face again. He remembered being five and playing with the sacks in the shearing shed. Dad was shearing the sheep, sweating and focused, and Mum and Gramp were stuffing wool into sacks. Dylan used to play in the sacks, hiding inside one, and peering out of the tiny gaps, pretending he was inside a giant Shreddie. He had known that one day, when he was grown up, he would be shearing and later on, when he was old, he'd be stuffing sacks. Now it looked like he might never even be a teenager. His heart battered away, as if it was trying to get out of his chest, never mind the sacking. What he needed, he thought desperately, was a way of making things better. Not a plan exactly, just something, anything that would slow things down and buy a bit more time and maybe find even the tiniest way to change things.

Out of the corner of his eye he saw a small tear in the sacking. It wasn't much, but he nosed the sack around until one eye saw out of it clearly. Faces. There. He was wrong about never seeing a face again. Already things were improving.

Or maybe not. Floyd was getting the same treatment, bundled into a sack. Miss Crassy was serious. This was going to happen. They would be thrown into the river. The water would rush through the tiny holes and he would fight it and struggle. Then he would drown. He would be eaten by piranhas. He had seen those teeth and knew that there wouldn't be anything left of him to find except – what did Lucia call it? – sorry clean bones. His mother would never know what had happened to him.

'Where's my son, you madwoman?' Mac's voice had cracks in it, but it boomed out and echoed in the vast dome.

How much longer did they have before Anton threw them in the river? Was there anything he could say that would change her mind?

'Oh, don't worry about your son,' Miss Crassy said in a strong confident voice. 'He has been fed the best food, given exactly the right amount of exercise and sleep and read the most delightful stories. I have been most pernickety about that.' At that moment a doggy yowl, a 'yaroo!' went up somewhere back among the stacks of cages. 'He was exactly the right age for our … project. We have others, but they have been less well fed in infancy and have already aged beyond their years. I've finished with him now, but your boy was the perfect specimen. You should be proud of him.'

'*Specimen? Was?*' Mac howled. If you had to say which of them was mad, Dylan thought – the howling man with wild hair and bulging eyes, or the beautiful woman with the calm voice, you'd choose the wrong one. What did she mean by 'project'? And 'specimen'? She wasn't … she couldn't…?'

At that moment, through the slit in the sacking, Dylan saw Lucia at the end of an aisle, or at least, he saw her bare feet. The rest of her had disappeared behind Pernickety, who was in her arms, a great Scooby Doo of a dog, enthusiastically licking her ears.

She might have good, rich molasses running through her veins, but still she would leave. She would take Pernickety and go back to the main field camp, leaving him and Floyd tied up in sacks. She would take the motor boat and go downriver, away from Miss Crassy and this terrible place. He didn't even blame her. There was nothing she could do to help him that wouldn't get her killed as well. She was right. Her world was dangerous, and her best hope of surviving was to look after herself and no one else.

Even if she found some signal and emailed the photos from the field camp before she left, it would be too late to save him and Floyd and Mac and Joe. His mother would know what had happened to him. That might actually be worse.

The two orange heels began to swivel round. In fractions of a second, Miss Crassy would see Lucia. This was the one tiny moment in which Dylan could make a difference. This was why it was worth trying not to panic.

'Why will Mac be proud of Joe?' Dylan called out. 'What wonderful thing are you working on?'

The two orange heels turned back towards Dylan. 'I don't suppose it matters if you know,' she said. You could hear the excitement in her voice. 'Tell them to assemble the samples,' she said to Anton, and as soon as she spoke, Dylan saw the hem of a white coat move towards a cabinet and heard the clink of small bottles.

Miss Crassy announced, 'These young creatures are helping us to develop a regenerative anti-toxin that prolongs life. By decades.' She walked over to the jars of grey paste and tapped one with a long, painted nail. 'Fifty years at least! Algae from sloths' fur combined with bone marrow from young creatures creates an extraordinary paste which regenerates tissue and bone. We've tried using bone marrow from puppies and stray kids and it's quite cool. But the bone marrow of such a specimen as Joe...' she looked up to the top of the dome and shook her lovely hair so that it shimmered. 'Such a well-fed, clean specimen. He will be the prototype. Bone marrow from him, now that we've extracted it, can be reproduced many times over and marketed.'

As Miss Crassy talked, Dylan wriggled round and watched Lucia's bare feet pass aisle after aisle until she came level with what looked like the main entrance, which probably led to the track. Then they disappeared. With them went the last beautiful thing Dylan would ever see. Two bare feet. The bare feet of a friend who was leaving him – had to leave him – he understood that – to meet his death. He would never see her again, never hear her funny ideas in her odd words. Sadness crawled over every millimetre of his skin like a blanket of ants. They had only been friends for two days, but he knew that if he lived, he would want to know her for the rest of his life.

Miss Crassy's clear voice was still going on. 'And how many people will want that? Imagine!' She stroked her cheek and shook her mane of golden hair. 'Oh, it will be expensive of course. Only the very wealthy will be able to afford it. How much do you think all this has cost? And the difficulty of hiding it.'

Now Dylan understood what it was that ran in her veins. It *was* watery and coloured. That innocent, watery-looking purple liquid that dad used to clean paint off paintbrushes. So poisonous, Dad had said, that it destroys everything it touches. One gulp would rot your gut from the inside, dissolving the flesh, make you go blind and probably die. And if it didn't actually kill you,

you would wish it had. Methylated spirits. Tochi was right. There were evil spirits here. That was exactly what she had. How had he not sensed how powerful it was on the plane?

She frowned. 'You were such a nuisance, Mac,' she complained, as if she were talking to a muddy dog. 'Checking and double-checking everything. I employed you because you weren't a big name. I thought you would be so grateful to get the job that you wouldn't ask any questions. Just a small town conservationist from a bit of a country tacked on to little old England. I thought you'd roll over and do whatever I said. But you turned out to be more dedicated than the top guy I could have got from London or New York. I thought I'd made a terrible mistake. Until I saw your kid. Then I realised that your appointment was better than I hoped in the first place.' She sounded as if she was smiling, as if she was paying Mac a compliment.

Mac's feet kicked out, and he made a noise of utter digust.

Dylan had one more tiny desperate idea. He couldn't see how it would save them, but it might be one small piece of information which helped. He wriggled round to face Miss Crassy, nosed the tear in the sacking back into place and asked his question.

'Where is Joe?' Dylan asked. 'Can we see him?'

Miss Crassy shot a quick nervous glance behind her and took a step to the left, as if she was blocking everyone's glance from something. It was exactly the sort of guilty movement Tommo made when he didn't want you to find the last sweets he had hidden under his pillow.

'It would upset the project if he saw you. He must be kept entirely stress free and happy for the experiments to work.'

'You're insane.' Mac's voice was quiet now and reasonable. 'Experiments on kids. No one has ever, ever, done anything as wrong and mad as this throughout history and expected the world to be glad about it.'

Miss Crassy stepped close to Mac and leaned towards him so that her face almost touched his.

'Oh, but that's where you're wrong. That's what you've never understood. There is no end to the world's desire for longer life. A few articles might question my methods, but the money I make from the products will be more than enough to silence the newspapers. Oh, the advertising! The billboards!' She gazed up at the domed ceiling and stretched her arms out. 'Your son's face, thirty feet high, on flashing advertisements in Times Square in New York! Piccadilly Circus in London! Red Square in Moscow! The Arc de Triomphe in Paris! "Feel this young again," they'll say!' she cried, pulling her thumb and forefinger across in front of her, as if her words would be written under Joe's face. 'People won't care where this anti-toxin came from, once they see what it can do. They'll think his face is the face of a boy model with lovely skin and clear eyes. Not of the exquisite donor himself.'

'And when I'm Global Head of Special Projects, just think how I can develop this and other ideas. The wealthy already pay vast sums to live longer and look more beautiful. I will be the inventor of the best products in the world.' She seemed to see something that they couldn't. A vision, maybe, of a world with a few strangely beautiful people in it. 'My discovery will be as important as the discovery of penicillin, as going to the moon. My lecture at the conference this afternoon will be quoted like the speeches of Churchill, the Gettysburg address, the…'

Something distracted her and she cocked her head, listening.

Dylan listened too. A faint rumbling sound, growing louder, pierced the silence. It became even louder, a constant thrumming, and the dark shadows of hundreds of birds passed over the white dome above their heads.

TWENTY-SIX

The thunderous rumble became a terrible creaking. The white walls and ceiling shifted, seem to stretch and pull as if something enormous was yanking at them. The metal backbone of the great tent wobbled and the ribs twisted. A great snap sounded as the white plastic sheeting ripped apart and shrank away, exposing the bones of the tent. One huge rib buckled and broke in the middle and both new ends shot upwards as the sheeting fell in wrinkles to the ground.

What sort of monster could chew up such a lab? The flapping, shrinking plastic sheeting was hiding it from view. The sheeting rustled and contorted as it was sucked further and further into the jaws of...

The yellow digger.

It emerged from behind the sheeting, the caterpillar

treads trapping the white plastic and pulling it in as it moved forwards. The digger bucket was heaped full of tins and tools and standing up at the controls were Lucia and Pernickety, charging directly down the wide central space, towards the tables and sinks and apparatus.

Dylan's heart ballooned and burst. Crazy, brave, wonderful, insane Lucia! She had remembered everything! Fear and pride tumbled about inside Dylan like clothes in Mum's washing machine. And there was happiness in there, too; she hadn't just taken the motor boat and gone with Pernickety.

On and on came the digger. A table flew out of its way, chairs leapt into the air. It reached the long cabinet with the jars on and pushed it forwards and sideways. Jars smashed to the floor and something like cold grey custard oozed out.

Miss Crassy was screaming at Anton to do something and Anton was dancing, in his grey suit, literally dancing, arms up, legs bouncing, towards and then away from the digger as it came grumbling towards them.

'Back up!' yelled Dylan to Floyd and Mac, showing them what he meant by rolling away in his sack, leaving Lucia enough space to get past them. They shifted out of her path and then stopped, like an audience in a cinema, pinned to the spot to watch the madness unfold.

Miss Crassy, Anton and the technicians were crammed up against another cabinet, imprisoned by the oozing greyness on one side, and by shelves of barking puppies on the other. The digger came thundering onwards, only a few feet away now from the screaming huddle of people. Dylan stopped breathing. Miss Crassy and Anton scrabbled to get up on to the cabinet, grabbing onto each other and pulling each other off in their hurry to get up. They might be the worst grown-ups he had ever met – ever heard of, even – but he still didn't want to watch them being crushed under the digger's caterpillar treads.

'Stop!' he yelled, knowing perfectly well she couldn't hear him.

The digger jolted to a halt, its bucket jangling on its hinges, just inches from the scrunched-up group of technicians.

Miss Crassy, with one orange heel on Anton's shoulder, inched her way up to a sitting position on the cupboard, pointed at Lucia and screamed at Anton to do something. Lucia, sitting bolt upright, a queen on her throne, shifted some levers in the digger cabin and the bucket swung round to the right and tilted downwards, dropping all the tins and tools with a resounding clatter. Then it shot up again and did a scooping, tilting motion. Then it went down again, and up again and scooped again. A smile grew on Lucia's face and Dylan smiled with her. She had worked out how to control the bucket.

Then, as he watched, with a smooth, almost gentle movement, Lucia scooped Miss Crassy up from the top of the cabinet, raised the bucket to its highest height and turned off the engine. Two ankles and two high-heeled orange shoes kicked furiously over the edge of the bucket.

Anton jumped to his feet and dashed towards the digger. He climbed up the steps and flung open the cabin door. Lucia held Mac's phone up.

'Halt!' she cried. 'Listen! Lend me your lugholes! All photographs emailed to your list, DocMac,' she called.

'What?' came Miss Crassy's voice. She was now kneeling up in the bucket and peering down at them all. 'Anton! Get me down from here.'

'I take photographs of secret laboratory and puppies in cages while in meantime you are tussling with my esteemed Mac,' Lucia said. 'I send them to all the publications on your list, Mac. And the CEO of BlueBird. Photos of all staff emailed around world. All of you. I most supremely careful in this matter. I most thorough personage.'

'Don't be ridiculous. Who cares about a few dogs? We can prove that they've been fed. No one will print your story.'

'Ah, but problematics not only with puppies, is it, Missy Crassy? I already announced I was thorough.' Lucia pointed behind Miss Crassy, to the left. 'Over yonder are cages containing kids. Kids! And that,' she breathed in and drew herself up, 'is a scandalising travesty of the highest order. How the world respond to that?' The phone pinged as she spoke and she glanced at it, holding an arm out to stop Anton. 'Oh, regard, an email already. From the *Guardian* newspaper in London. What "expressing interest" mean, Missy Crossy?' Her phone pinged again and again. 'Ooooeee! *National Geographic* dispatches a photographer to Manaus,' she said.

Anton grabbed the phone off Lucia and tapped at it, his face reddening and his eyebrows creeping towards each other. He gave a horrible roar, flung the phone to the ground and sprinted off down the aisle towards the emergency exit tunnel. 'It's all over!' he yelled, filling the place with the sour stench of rancid cream. 'Get out of here quick!' He repeated himself in Portuguese and the technicians, every single one of them, stopped cowering. They leapt up and ran after him, all disappearing past the plastic strips that had served as a door to the tunnel.

'Anton?' shrieked Miss Crassy, her golden hair still hanging in a perfect curtain around her face. 'You addle-headed coot! Come back! If you'd only taken care of that boy, as I explicitly told you to do, none of this would have happened!'

Lucia leaped off the digger, grabbed something from the cabin and ran behind Mac and Dylan and Floyd to cut open the sacks.

As the sacking fell away, Dylan rose slowly to his feet to see Lucia standing right in front of him in her bare feet, sticky-up fringe and muddy shorts. He threw his arms around her and hugged her tight, feeling her bony shoulders. He would never, ever, however long he lived, not be friends with her, not know where she was and how she was.

'You came back,' he said, gulping. 'They were going to drown us. You saved our lives.' He pushed her away gently, embarrassed.

Lucia shrugged. 'I never see a grown-up do anything for anyone till I meet SirMacDoc. This foolish kindness – possibly contagious.' But she was grinning the biggest grin and she glanced at Dylan sideways.

'Joe?' called Mac, weakly, still sitting in his chair, one arm cradling the other.

'He'll be over there,' Dylan said. 'Behind where Miss Crassy was standing. Over to the left.' Now that he was out of the sacking, and Miss Crassy was in a digger bucket, out of the way, Dylan felt supremely powerful. Now he could make everything right again. H knew exactly what to do. He, Floyd and Lucia shot off between the cages, then stopped.

These cages held kids.

Stacked three high, with a rough blanket each and only enough room to curl up in. A boy or girl in each one. Scruffy, squatting and peering out. Floyd drew back the bolt on the first one, who scrabbled backwards into a corner.

'Ay, Meu Dios,' Lucia said, 'OK, todos OK.' She gesticulated at them to come out and slowly they moved towards the front of their cages as the bolts slid back, one after the other. Dylan joined in, slamming the bolts back,

218

smiling at the kids, encouraging them to come out. At Lucia's voice they came alive, calling out in fast Portuguese which she answered like rapid bullet fire back at them. All of them were asking questions and answering them for each other and explaining and Lucia was explaining louder than anyone else. They climbed down from their cages and stretched themselves like animals. Then they jumped up and down and started running about, hugging each other. They crowded round Lucia and the cry went up, 'Lucia! Ay que geant!'

They lifted her up, chanting her name, carrying her along like a mascot, as if she had freed them single-handedly. Dylan noticed that Floyd was still darting from cage to cage, flinging open doors that were already open, calling for Joe.

'Lucia,' yelled Dylan above the noise. 'Ask them where Joe is. The Welsh boy. The one who speaks English. Floyd's brother, looks just like him. Where is he? We still haven't found him.'

Lucia gabbled away, arms all over the place, pointing to Floyd, showing Joe's height. The kids grew quiet, and serious expressions came on their faces. One or two shook their heads and mumbled something.

'She removed him away,' Lucia said. 'He's installed somewhere different. He was special,' she said, stroking Pernickety who was leaning up against her leg as if he'd been stuck there with superglue.

One of the kids pointed to the far end of what was left

of the laboratory, where a plastic door was still intact and the sheeting wall was only partly ripped up.

'This boy says she took him thereabouts,' Lucia said.

Floyd and Dylan shot off towards the door and ripped it open. With a shock, Dylan remembered they were still in the rainforest, still miles and miles from anywhere. Trees surrounded them but a clear path led the way forwards through the dark tangle. Floyd ran off and Dylan followed. Miss Crassy's words came back to him 'we've finished with him'. Could it already be too late? More sun filtered down through the trees as the path came out to an end. The laboratory had been hidden from the river by only a thin margin of trees.

From the end of the path it was only a short way to a small wooden house on stilts. Or not so much a house as a large room with a balcony. It had been built to look out over the Amazon and could be reached by a long ladder. Floyd flew up the ladder with Dylan following. Floyd burst through the door and stopped.

Over Floyd's shoulder, Dylan glimpsed a high ceilinged room painted in rainbow colours. Bean bags were scattered over thick carpet, and a hammock, filled with cushions, hung from wooden poles. A fridge with a glass door was full of fruit and plates of food. The only unpleasant thing was a sink and table with the same sort of apparatus Dylan had seen in the laboratory. With all the colour and unexpected decorations, it was a few moments before Dylan noticed an extremely pale young boy lying on a beanbag in the corner. He had huge bandages around each thigh, but apart from that, he could have been a miniature version of Floyd, right there in front of them.

Floyd rushed to his side and touched his arm.

'Joe?' he said.

The boy didn't move. His face was chalky white and his lips, slightly open, were nearly blue. His body was stone-still. Dylan stared at his chest, willing it to move, but not able to detect even the slightest change.

Joe?' Floyd's voice was croaky. He lifted the boy's arm and stroked his hand. 'Joe?' His voice broke and crumbled. Floyd laid the hand gently back onto Joe's chest. His shoulders shook. 'Joe?' This time Floyd's voice was high and thin and hopeless.

The small body shuddered.

'Joe? It's Floyd. I've come to take you home.'

Slowly, the eyelids opened. The boy's dull eyes locked on to Floyd's for what seemed like forever. Then one slim arm reached up towards Floyd's neck and Floyd bent forwards into the hug, his own arms outstretched to gather up the small body. Dylan breathed again, turned on his heel and went out to the balcony, blinking away the wetness in his eyes.

When his vision had cleared, he saw that beyond the path was the river itself, the broad, bronze-brown, breathless Amazon river, a massive magical murmuring body of water, a river so wide and so slow you could spend the rest of your life looking at it and still not have enough time. Smells of life and death, of fresh greenery, of rotting brownery, of the upwardness of birds and the secrecy of fish, of possibility and excitement invaded Dylan's senses. The sky was higher and wider than any sky in Wales, with a horizon that drifted off so far that Dylan's mind stretched just thinking about it. It stretched and stretched until it burst, and everything Dylan had understood until now had to reorganise itself, like a kaleidoscope turned into a different pattern. This must be what people meant by expanding your mind. Dylan's place by the river was everything to him, but it was not everything. Ideas about life and the world and all the rivers and what he would do and where he would go sparked off in his brain like fireworks. He had stopped wanting to save his farm and his patch by the river. He wanted to save every patch, by every river.

The boys carried Joe carefully down the ladder. They emptied a wheelbarrow full of tinned peaches and ran up to bring a beanbag down. By the time they'd settled him into the wheelbarrow and given him a juice, he was falling asleep again. It was Dylan's first chance to look at Joe closely. He looked exactly like Floyd, only with a softer face. Big brown eyes, dark hair, pale skin. Dylan tried to see what Miss Crassy had been going on about, the 'lovely' skin, the 'clear' eyes, but Joe looked pretty ordinary to him. Just like Tommo, with that hopeful look that a bag of sweets might be around the corner.

TWENTY-SEVEN

Back inside the crumpled dome, every cage had been flung open and each kid had puppies in their arms, on their lap, or sprawled over their stomach, a moving sea of puppies of every shade of white and black and brown and grey. Lucia was opening tin after tin from the pile and handing them out to the kids who shared them with their puppies. Pernickety lay asleep next to Lucia, all legs and greyness. Miss Crassy was still kneeling up in the digger bucket, yelling, trying to be heard over the noise and excitement. They all fell quiet – even Miss Crassy – as Dylan and Floyd approached with Joe in the wheelbarrow.

Mac remained in his chair, grey-faced, holding his left arm. When he saw Joe he held his right arm out and Floyd wheeled Joe close so that they could have a half-hug. Tears poured down Mac's face.

'Problematic silence,' Lucia said, and everyone looked away.

Eventually Mac spoke.

'We both need medical attention,' he said, through gritted teeth. 'But Joe needs it urgently. He needs a doctor. Now.' He gazed around at the group of kids, puppies, and Miss Crassy high up in the bucket, as if hoping one of them could produce a doctor.

'Get me down from here, Mac, and I'll give him all the medicine he needs. In fact, let's do a deal. You can join me in my business – I can pay you handsomely, you'll be rich. Just get these wretched kids to lower me down. No one will believe those photos are real. You know that.'

'Oh, put a sock in it, Crasso,' Mac said, wearily. 'You're a criminal and you're going to jail. Society needs to be protected from people like you.' He tried to stand up. 'Harrrrr!' he yowled as his left arm moved.

'A few of us could go to Manaus and get help,' Dylan said.

'I'm not strong enough,' Mac whispered.

'I am,' Dylan and Lucia said in unison.

They glanced at each other and grinned.

'Dad, that's what we'll do. We'll go for help,' Floyd said. 'We'll take Joe to Manaus.'

'On your own? That's an insane idea,' Mac said, but his voice was weak now and his eyes kept closing.

'No!' Shrieked Miss Crassy. 'No one will believe you

anyway. Who's going to listen to a few raggedy kids like you?'

'No, listen, Dad. We can't leave Joe here. He'll get to a doctor much quicker if we take him. We can't just wait around for people to come.'

'There's a motor boat at the field camp. Lucia's got the key. It's probably just like driving a digger,' Dylan said.

'Possibly exist a manual,' Lucia said, her eyes lighting up.

'Wait.' Slowly, and wincing with each word, Mac spoke. 'You're right, Joe needs to get out of here. I get the feeling you lot could run the world if you had to. But listen to one piece of advice before you go.' He stopped and closed his eyes.

'Yes?' Dylan asked.

'You're right. It's not hard to turn the engine on and steer the boat. The difficult thing will be stopping. Turn the engine off long before you get to the dock, OK? Boats don't stop straight away. They keep on going. Just don't want you to crash.' Mac opened his eyes again.

'And I need to speak to Lucia.'

Lucia shot up to where he sat. 'Yes, Sir DocMac?'

'Thank you,' he said, fixing her with a stare, 'for telling the world and thank you for coming back. It's not much, but I'd like you to keep my phone. I wish I had more to give.'

'Yes, SirMacDocMacSir,' she said, gulping.

'What about Miss Crassy?' Dylan asked. Miss Crassy's

225

eyes were shut, but her lips moved and eyebrows were knitted together furiously. Her head gave constant tiny shakes, tiny repeated 'no's.

'Cruddy Crossy Missy Crassy,' Lucia said, and they all laughed.

'She can wait here with us. Lucia, tell the kids they must not hurt her.' Lucia translated and the kids looked disappointed. 'I mean it. She absolutely must not be hurt or even frightened. We will not stoop to her behaviour.' Then a look of mischief flashed across his contorted face. 'Unless she tries anything silly. In which case she can work out for herself how to get away from a herd of angry kids.'

Mac gave Joe one more hug, then fell back in his chair, his face creased with pain.

'Best depart instantly,' Lucia said.

'Come on, Joe,' Floyd said.

The three of them waved goodbye as Floyd wheeled Joe towards what had been the main entrance of the laboratory, where the track began.

Dylan worked out that their flight would be leaving from Salvador in nine hours. He made rough calculations in his head. He reckoned there was about a one in a thousand chance of getting it. Best not to even think about it.

As they passed the central aisle, Dylan noticed the sloth move one arm slowly up to its chest. So it wasn't dead. He put a hand on its shoulder and it opened its eyes. It might take the sloth days to find a munguba tree from the centre of the destroyed lab, and it would already be hungry. He gathered it up in his arms and felt the sloth's rough fur, the sharpness of its hard claws, and the stillness in its body. It smelled like Pernickety had, sort of deliciously sweet and comforting.

Dylan led the way, carrying the sloth, a heavy, scratchy weight which shifted now and then. Floyd and Lucia wheeled Joe, who slept, and Pernickety trotted along beside them.

Halfway along the track, Dylan spotted a munguba tree with its sticky white mop heads and large red baubles. With the sloth still clinging to his neck, Dylan carefully climbed over the fence into the forest. The sloth's gentle face looked as if it was smiling, and it seemed to be hugging him, but Dylan knew it was a creature he could never understand. Dylan unlooped its arms from around his neck and replaced them around the trunk of the munguba tree. By the time he had climbed back over the fence, the sloth was reaching one arm slowly up towards the lowest branch, and Dylan said a silent goodbye.

The field camp was deserted. The cargo boat had gone. Only the motor boat and the canoe were left, and Lucia took the key out of her pocket and dangled it happily.

Dylan and Lucia clambered onto the boat and into the cockpit. They rushed out again a moment later with cushions and helped Floyd lift Joe onto them. When he was comfortable, they made a more careful search.

'I found the ignition!' Dylan called.

Lucia held up a dirty, battered book. 'And instructions in seven languages! I learn Russian on way home!'

TWENTY-EIGHT

Lucia yelled instructions from the manual and Dylan turned the key in the ignition and pressed the starter button. Between them, they had the boat running in minutes. Dylan had to stand on an old beer crate to see over the top of the steering wheel, but making it go wasn't difficult. Turning it round was the tricky bit: they set off in reverse and crashed into one side of the creek, then bumped the other side gently. But that was just like driving the tractor or digger for the first time. You were all over the place for a few minutes, but you got the hang of it pretty quickly. Before long they were off, down the dark creek, into the twilight under the heavy canopy. Soon after that they came to the creek's mouth and out into sunshine.

Dylan steered the boat out into the huge expanse of the

river while Lucia continued to read the manual with Pernickety not so much on her lap, as on all of her. Floyd sat with Joe's head in his lap, murmuring to him. Dylan gazed at the river, unwilling to waste a second of this journey looking anywhere else.

A great peace settled in Dylan's chest. On and on they motored, the engine a quiet hum under the water, and no other sounds apart from the odd splash of fish or the calling of a bird.

Saving the farm was impossible, but a new emotion was washing through him and Dylan thought it might be pride. He and Floyd had succeeded in rescuing Mac and Joe and even in saving loads of kids, dogs and a sloth. And they had stopped Miss Crassy's 'scandalising travesty of the highest order'. Even the worry of missing the plane and asking his dad to pay hundreds of pounds to get him home couldn't spoil that. In fact, he didn't think anything could ever spoil that, for as long as he lived. They had the whole river to themselves and it spread out before him like his whole life, huge, unmapped, teeming with possibility and mystery. OK, so he hadn't managed to save *his* river and *his* farm, but as he looked out over the Amazon he thought – if the whole world had rivers all over it, maybe the whole world was just one big farm. Maybe Gramp was wrong, as well as being right. Everywhere was incredibly different, but it was sort of the same as well.

So if the whole world was a farm, he could never really

move away from it. And if here, in Manaus and up the Amazon he had made friends, and found a way to achieve something, and if hundreds of mosquitos were flying around with his blood in them, or being enjoyed and digested by toucans, if bits of his blood were flying around in the rainforest and Tochi and Lucia were his friends, and if sometimes, just sometimes, the rain falling on the rainforest came from Aberdovey and the lake behind Cader Idris – then maybe the whole world was home, too?

After about two hours, they came across other boats on the river. People from a tourist boat waved to him, and closer to the shoreline were a couple of kids doing backflips off a tree trunk. A bird of prey patrolled a patch of water ahead, stopping to hover, head down, every now and then. It dived, opening its beak as it hit the water. There was a splash and struggle, then it flapped furiously and rose up, a silvery fish caught in its beak. If only his dad could see him now, skipper of a speed boat, about to get help for Mac and all the kids.

He began to think there might even be other ways to live his life. If he couldn't be a sheep farmer, he could be a bat specialist, a speed-boat driver, a conservationist like Mac, a nut farmer, a sloth doctor, a teacher of slang, a dog trainer... One way or another he'd definitely find something to do that he loved.

After another hour of quiet and space and the rich woody smells of the huge river beneath them, Lucia closed the manual and stared out over the water.

'I receive signal again here,' she said, tapping into Mac's phone. 'Ooh, so many messages! But first, I discover meaning of your name.' She tapped away and gazed at the screen. 'Ha! You are never guessing! Dylan was godly hero! Welsh myths say it. Sea-hero. "Dy" is meaning "great" and – how you say this funny bunch of letters?'

Dylan glanced at the phone and saw 'llanw'. 'Sort of "Clannoo",' he said.

'Meaning "flow". So, "great flow". Or in low register, slangy talk, "big river",' Lucia said.

'Does that mean … my name is river?' Dylan asked. 'That's odd,' and he turned back to look over the moving expanse of the Amazon.

TWENTY-NINE

The river grew busier. Lucia kept watch and called out to Dylan to mind a canoe, or go left to get out of the path of a huge passenger steamer. At last, the docks of Manaus were in sight. As they drew closer Dylan was able to smell them: the rich smells of fish and engine oil, and the dry dusty smell of hemp rope dragged against wood. An excited knot of men and women with cameras had gathered round someone and Dylan was sure he heard the name of 'BlueBird' being shouted more than once.

Dylan aimed for a space between two tourist boats and, remembering Mac's advice, cut the engine a little way from the dock. The boat drifted on and bumped into the side, making Dylan and Lucia grab at the boat's woodwork. Immediately a man with a big camera ran towards them, gabbling.

'He hopeful to hire my boat,' Lucia said.

'Lucia, really it belongs to BlueBird, we can't hire it out.' The moment Dylan said the word 'BlueBird', the photographer gasped and rushed back towards the crowd, shouting and waving his arms around. This had a strange effect. The whole knot of people undid itself and followed the photographer back to where Dylan and Floyd were tying the boat onto the dock. From the middle of the crowd, Mustafa Shadid emerged, a head taller than everyone else. A woman in a suit stood behind him, holding two phones and a clipboard.

'Sir,' she said. 'Call from the government. Agricultural department.'

'Not just now, Dolores. I'm gathering intelligence. I'll speak to them when I know more.' He turned to Dylan and Lucia.

'Goodness. You two again. Have you been sending prank emails about BlueBird?

'No, Sir,' Dylan said.

'Yes, Sir,' Lucia said.

The CEO frowned and his eyes glittered.

'I will have you arrested if...'

'She doesn't know the word "prank", sir. We've just come from the BlueBird field camp.'

'And you have some story to tell me, no doubt.'

'Yes,' Dylan said, and heard, 'yes', 'yes', behind him from Lucia and Floyd.

'Explain yourselves,' the CEO said. 'I listen to every

single complaint. If BlueBird wasn't the world's most transparent, most ethically conscious company I'd be worried about that email and those photos. That field camp is a natural clearing. Not a single tree had to be cut down there. I pride myself on that. All our waste is taken away from the site and brought back here to Manaus. We aim to leave the area exactly as we found it. Hot, sweaty, teeming with life. So we need to get this allegation cleared up immediately.'

Everyone was silent, all eyes were on Dylan.

'There's a lot to tell,' he said.

'Begin then.' Mr Shadid sat himself down on a wooden crate, and folded his arms. Dylan was confused. Surrounded by dozens of photographers and journalists, Mr Shadid seemed perfectly at ease. He had seen the email and the photos, so either he didn't believe they were true, or he just didn't care.

'The field camp wasn't the only area being used by BlueBird,' Dylan said.

'Seriously sizeable laboratory existing there,' Lucia said. Mr Shadid sighed.

'Yes, there's a small laboratory there,' he said. 'Not much bigger than a greenhouse. We're cultivating several species of ferns and other plants.'

'No, this was bigger than ... the Manaus Opera House. With a huge white dome.'

Mr Shadid frowned. 'We're talking about the clearing near the creek, aren't we?'

'No!' cried Dylan, Lucia and Floyd all at once.

'It's a lab!'

'It's right in the jungle!'

'With test tubes and experiments! And cages!'

The woman with the clipboard stepped forward and spoke loudly, so the press could hear.

'Then this has nothing to do with BlueBird. We don't use animals in our experiments.'

'Wait, Dolores. It is not my intention to hide anything. We need to understand exactly what these kids think they saw before we start denying things.' He turned to Dylan. 'You're trying to tell me there is a real laboratory there? Apart from the field camp?'

'Yes,' Dylan said, 'there's a hidden pathway beyond the field camp. Dozens and dozens of trees have been cut down.'

Mr Shadid jerked as if someone had stuck him in the side with a pin. 'That is an extremely serious allegation. Every single tree is a city,' he said. 'With hundreds of creatures living in it, sheltering in it, living off it. Jaguars, sloths, monkeys, parrots, honey bears. Lizards, chameleons, tree frogs. Woodlice, moths, beetles, ants, butterflies. Vines, tree-ferns, epiphytes, lichens, algae, liverworts and mosses. Never mind the fungi. If any of BlueBird's employees did this without permission, they would be fired immediately.'

Dylan and Lucia grinned.

'But I would need a lot more evidence than these

photos and you kids spinning me a story. The photos could have been taken anywhere. If this is a publicity stunt for some…'

'It gets worse, sir,' Dylan said.

Mr Shadid pursed his lips and folded his arms. 'Indeed?' he said.

'Listen!' cried Lucia. She held up Mac's phone and Miss Crassy's voice came tinnily out of it. 'Wait!' She rushed into the cockpit and brought out an empty mug. She placed the phone in it, held the mug up high and started the recording again. This time the voice came out louder.

'*These young creatures are helping us develop a regenerative anti-toxin that prolongs life.*' Here there was the tapping noise of Miss Crassy's fingernails. '*We've tried using bone marrow from puppies and stray kids and it's quite cool. But the bone marrow of such a specimen as Joe…*' Lucia turned it off.

'By all that is sacred,' Mr Shadid breathed. 'Miss Crassy.'

'My brother is here, sir. Joe,' called Floyd from the boat. Mr Shadid walked to the edge of the dock and peered in at Joe, who was lying back, pale and barely able to open his eyes. Then Mr Shadid sat back on the crate and melted a little.

As Dylan and Lucia described the secret laboratory and gave more and more details confirming that the photos were of a BlueBird project, Mr Shadid sank into himself. When they described just how many puppies were in cages, his mouth fell open. When they told him about the kids, and how ragged and thin they were, it snapped shut again. 'This has all been done in BlueBird's name by Miss Crassy?' he asked, in a voice as cold and hard as steel. Lucia showed him more photos on the phone. His face reddened right up to the roots of his hair as he stared at them. For a long while he didn't move.

Dylan and Lucia looked at each other.

'Sir?' Dylan said.

Mr Shadid stiffened his shoulders.

'Are the children safe now?'

'Yes, they're with Mac. He's got a broken arm.'

'Mac Adams? You came across him?'

'He's my dad, sir,' Floyd said, proudly.

'He tried to tell me about this and I thought he was ill.' Mr Shadid shook his head. 'Mac risked his job – maybe his life – to investigate this.'

He stood up and addressed the crowd of journalists.

'I don't know how much of this story you have heard, but we are now taking it very seriously indeed. We will investigate immediately. We will be publicising every last detail of it as soon as we are sure of the facts. At the moment we only know there is an allegation of…' he took a deep breath, 'what can only be called an atrocity committed in BlueBird's name. It is possible that the rainforest, wildlife, animals and…' here he closed his eyes for a moment, 'even children have been harmed. If it is true, it will take decades to repair the damage, but we will rehome every child and replace every tree. We will clear every last trace of this horrific laboratory from the Amazon. Every rivet, every nail, every scrap of plastic. Nothing unnatural will be left behind.'

'In fact,' he summoned two of his staff, 'Call the police. Give them and the press all the help they need. And get me supplies for a trip to the fieldcamp. We'll take this boat as soon as we're ready.' He stood up and sat down again. He shook his head and looked at Floyd. 'Your poor brother and father. And all those poor children and sloths and dogs. And all those beautiful trees,' he said.

Journalists crowded round him, but he fought his way out and came back to shake Dylan and Lucia and Floyd vigorously by the hand.

'Thank you, thank you. You three have done a truly remarkable thing. I must go upriver immediately, but what do you kids need now? My office can organise everything.'

'Well,' Dylan said, 'Joe needs medical attention.'

'And I'm not leaving him behind,' Floyd said.

'And Lucia wants to go to a school.' Dylan did a 'weirdo' face at her.

'And what about you, boy, what do you want?' asked Mr Shadid, looking Dylan straight in the eye.

'Our flights leave from Salvador in five hours,' Dylan said. 'I don't suppose you've got a spare car, a doctor and one of those small planes that go straight away, have you?'

'Not asking about your farm anymore?'

'No, sir,' Dylan said, feeling heat creep up his neck. 'I get it now.'

Mr Shadid turned to his assistant.

'Dolores, I want you personally to find a doctor, ask if Joe can travel, and if so, arrange flights, and everything else needed to get these kids home safely. I'll sign a form for them to fly home accompanied and I'll email it to Salvador airport. And find a school that can take,' he thought for a moment, 'dozens of children. Or build one. Do whatever you have to do. And I want a full investigation of how such a thing could possibly happen in my company.' He turned to Dylan. 'As for you – I want you to write it all down for me – everything, right from the beginning. Leave nothing out and get it done on the flight. I'll expect it by the end of tomorrow.'

Dolores tapped on her phone and spoke quietly into it, making call after call. She didn't sound bossy enough to Dylan to get anything done, but a doctor turned up within minutes to examine Joe. The doctor's serious face relaxed into a smile as she confirmed that Joe was well enough to travel, and that she would be delighted to accompany him to England as she had an aunt there she hadn't seen for years. A private plane was waiting for them at Manaus airport, Dolores said.

Floyd hugged Lucia so tightly that Dylan thought her bones would break.

'Thank you for coming back to rescue us,' he said, and turned away to hold Joe's hand again.

Dylan and Lucia looked at each other, then looked away again.

'Farewell,' she said.

'Bye,' Dylan said, awkwardly.

'I surmise that we will not be meeting again.'

'We will,' Dylan said. 'I'm coming back. It might be a while, but I'm definitely coming back.'

She nodded, and looked even crosser. She took a deep breath and her eyes filled with tears.

'I am loving you, 'fraid so,' she whispered.

Dylan gulped. He opened his mouth and closed it again.

'Yes,' he said, and then more certainly, 'yes'.

THIRTY

In the small plane, the BlueBird doctor made Joe comfortable and pointed to a fridge full of food to Dylan and Floyd. Dylan glanced at the ceiling and the walls. They were just far away enough for the burning in his stomach to settle down.

As they took off from Manaus airport the cars and houses turned from normal size to toy size to invisible. The enormous width of the Amazon river shrank and the individual trees began to be lost in the thick green carpet. Dylan looked back as far as he could out of the tiny window to where the river narrowed and split off into tributaries. He had been deep in the heart of that forest, part of that wilderness.

'Goodbye for now,' he whispered. 'I will come back one day.'

It wasn't until they reached Salvador airport and the doctor and Joe were on the plane and Floyd was fussing around with his phone and charger that Dylan began to feel sweaty and hot and cold and shivery and sick. How had he got through this flight before? He managed three steps into the plane when his feet stopped obeying him. Yet again Floyd had to shove him in the back to make him keep walking. Floyd was waffling on about how he would show Joe the bike track and the river and how he hoped Joe and Tommo would get on well and how his mum was going to be so happy and jokey again, when he stopped abruptly.

'You look a bit funny. You alright?'

Dylan's vision was shrinking and he couldn't breathe. He tried to keep shuffling along the aisle but he couldn't make much progress.

'Keep talking,' he said, through clenched teeth. He tried to think of the Amazon and the wide open skies, but all he could see was the narrow aisle, the tiny windows and the roof just a few inches above his head.

'What's the matter?'

'Just – keep – talking.'

'Are you going to be sick? Chunder up?'

Dylan's vision began to go black and his heart beat more and more loudly. All the liquids in his body seemed to have got muddled up. His mouth was dry and his palms were wet. He turned around to face Floyd. 'Get out of my way. I have to get off. I can't fly.'

'You have to, Dylan. If we don't take this plane it'll just be another. There isn't any other way to get home.'

'No, I can't, move! Get out of my way.' He tried backing into Floyd, but Floyd put a firm hand on his shoulders and pushed. Then Floyd started talking, in a steady, low voice. He told Dylan about his old school and the funny dinnerlady who wore different earrings every single day, sometimes tiny footballs, sometimes miniature space rockets, once a real oak leaf in each ear. He herded Dylan into the right seat, his voice never stopping, telling him about a tent his dad had made for him and Joe, and how they had slept in it one night and told each other ghost stories. About how two owls had called to each other in the night, in stereo, either side of the tent. He kept going as the plane began to taxi towards the runway, talked to him as the engine revved and the wings creaked. Told him about the time his mum made a cake that you nearly had to stand on the table with a saw to slice. Chainsaw cake, they called it, and now she just made biscuits for birthdays. Once they were in their seats, Dylan locked his eyes onto Floyd's as he talked. Dimly Dylan was aware that the plane had set off down the runway, that it was picking up speed and that it had lifted into the air, and that his hand hurt from gripping the arm rest so hard; but mainly he could see the playground from Floyd's old school that he was describing, with the strange concrete water tower and its huge yellow globe on top. The climbing frame with the monkey bars and the fact that each class had to take turns on different days of the week. It didn't matter what Floyd was saying. It just mattered that he was talking to him, that his voice gave him a lifeline and that Floyd was looking straight at him and that Dylan could breathe now and that the panic was shrinking instead of growing.

At last they were airborne and Dylan no longer had a choice. The ceiling seemed to be staying where it was, for the time being. He seemed to be able to breathe. He dried his palms on his trousers and swallowed.

'Thanks, mate. I'm OK now.'

'Why didn't you say you were afraid of flying? Why did you even think of flying to Brazil if it makes you feel that bad?'

'I didn't know. I was excited to fly. Then in the departure lounge at Birmingham I started thinking about how my dad was afraid of flying and my guts turned to boiling oil.'

'Family fears,' Floyd said. 'Mum says they're catching. I'm terrified of...' he whispered, 'cotton wool.'

'Of *cotton wool*?' Dylan had recovered almost enough to find this funny.

Floyd shuddered. 'Don't say it out loud. Horrible, dry, choking nightmare stuff. My Gran hates it. But I won't tell if you don't.'

Dylan managed a small, tight grin. 'It's a deal,' he said, and they shook on it.

'You know what, Dylan?'

'What?'

'You might not have saved your farm, but coming upriver with Lucia meant you did save Joe and Dad and me and all those kids and Pernickety and the sloth and all the other animals. In fact,' Floyd paused, 'you saved the world from Miss Crassy.' He sat up and laughed. 'You sort of saved the world, Dylan!'

Floyd wasn't making any sense, but at least he was still talking and that helped distract Dylan from all the plastic around him, squeezing his brain into a slimy paste. He swallowed.

'You know what you need to do now?' Floyd said.

'What?'

'Write to Mr Shadid. Like he said. While you can remember everything.'

Dylan shook his head. 'Impossible. I hate writing things. In my head everything's exciting, but it always looks so boring in sentences. And anyway, I'm OK with it now. I know there's worse things than moving off the farm. We'll be alright. I'll think of something else to do with my life.'

'Yeah, but it's not about that. You still have to write it. He asked you to.'

'I can't. I couldn't even start. I mean, I could tell Tommo what happened, dead easy, but it would have to be different for Mr Shadid, wouldn't it? It would have to be in serious paragraphs and stuff. With Lucia's weird words.'

'Tell the story to Tommo then. Here,' Floyd passed Dylan his phone. 'Write it on my phone, in texts. I know you can't send them from the plane, but you can save them to the phone. Then you can copy and paste them into a word document and email it to him. Just tell him everything that happened. You could edit it a bit when you get home. Hey – know what? It'll double up as the Geography project.'

Dylan pictured Tommo sitting on his top bunk, legs dangling, and him, Dylan, sitting opposite him. How would he tell him the story of BlueBird and the evil Miss Crassy? Tommo always listened. He never got bored. He always asked questions. Dylan could see himself, explaining it all to Tommo, telling it like an exciting story, building BlueBird up to be the best company in the world, then introducing all the suspicious things that Mac had described. Then describing exactly how he, Lucia and Floyd had discovered the lab and freed all the boys and puppies. He would tell how he had met the CEO and understood that there was a bigger picture.

So while Floyd watched a film about a guy trying to make a home on Mars, and kept checking on Joe, who just slept in his seat next to the doctor, Dylan tapped away with his thumbs on Floyd's phone. Every now and then he pressed 'send' and got a message back saying 'text not delivered'. But there it was, sliding upwards on the phone, with a red exclamation mark beside it and space for a new text message underneath. Dylan thumbed the keypad and wrote and wrote and wrote. He told Tommo everything, absolutely everything, from the time Floyd told him that Joe was scared, until now. Had they really only been away for five days?

After the meal and a sleep, Dylan woke in the night and read all the texts he had written. He had got the whole story down but there were a few places where he could see how to improve it with some of Lucia's words. He said nothing about the treehouse or his river, or how desperately he wanted to live his life on the farm, but he said it might be a squander of trees to cut some down, and added that the robin would be discombobulated when his bit of the river disappeared because of some diversion to create boggy land for moss. He said he really wasn't sure the robin would see the bigger picture. He worked all through the darkness while Floyd slept, concentrating so hard that the awful roof of the plane, just a few inches up, stayed where it was and didn't come pressing down on his head.

At Birmingham airport, before they went through customs, Floyd said goodbye to Joe and the doctor.

'Mum'll freak out if she knows I've been in Brazil with you. And Dylan's parents will probably lose it, too. We're all safe now, so it's best if Dylan and I travel back separately. Mum'll meet you the other side of customs – it's all arranged, and I'll see you at home. OK? We'll wait in a shop for half an hour to make sure she doesn't see us.'

Joe nodded. He was still weak, but his eyes were brighter and he smiled.

'You can come to the river, Joe,' Dylan said. 'My brother Tommo's the same age as you.'

Dylan and Floyd hung around Boots for a bit, then drifted off to WH Smiths. Dylan wandered around until the spine of a thick book caught his eye. THESAURUS, it said, vertically. Before his trip to Brazil he wouldn't even have noticed it, and the funny thing was that now, if he had any money, he would buy it. He was just wondering what Lucia was doing when his arm was yanked almost out of its socket.

'Look!' Floyd cried, dragging him over to the newspaper stand.

Lucia's face grinned at them from five different newspapers. She stood in the clearing by the field camp, next to Mustafa Shadid, hands on her hips. 'Homeless Girl Uncovers Atrocity' said one headline. 'Amazon Horror Revealed by Street Girl', said another.

The train drew in to Machynlleth station at three in the afternoon. It was just one hour until the coach came back from the trip. The boys took the back roads to the school playing fields and hid behind the games equipment shed.

'That talking thing you did on the plane,' Dylan said. 'That was pretty cool.'

'I worked it out with Mum. When she was sad after Dad and Joe left, I could only make her happy by talking. It worked like magic. She'd start off really gloomy, but if I kept going and kept looking at her, she'd come round. She'd be OK after a bit and make supper and we'd have a hug and then we'd carry on. She's going to be insanely happy to have Joe back. I bet she'll start dancing in the kitchen again when she's cooking, waving her wooden spoon around and trying to get Joe and me to join in. We used to groan when she did that.'

Just minutes before pick up time at the High School, Floyd's phone pinged manically with texts from Matt telling them the coach had come in a bit early and where were they? Because he couldn't cover for them much longer. As they ran around the corner of the games shed into the school car park, they saw Matt talking earnestly to Dylan's mum, blocking her way as she tried to reach the Geography teacher, who was standing by the coach with just one boy, looking around for his parent. As soon as they were in sight, Matt pointed to them, and Dylan's mother turned and saw him.

'Why did you come from over there?' she asked, hugging Dylan. 'And where's your rucksack?'

'We had to put something back for Mrs Hughes,' Floyd said, before Dylan could think.

'I left my rucksack behind, sorry,' Dylan said.

Dylan's mum's eyes narrowed.

'You've lost your whole rucksack? With everything in it?'

'It got a bit wrecked anyway. But I'll earn enough to pay for it all. I'll weed your whole polytunnel.'

'You've been up to something,' she said.

'Can we go now, Mum?' asked Dylan. 'I'm really tired.'

'I just want to say thank you to Mrs Hughes.'

'No, Mum, she says she hates that. She just wants to go home.'

'Really?' she looked doubtful.

'Yes. Hey Mum, I've done my geography project,' Dylan said. 'I just need to print it and it'll be ready to hand in.'

'Oh, well done, Dylan!' She beamed at him, then frowned again. 'Are you sure you haven't been up to something?'

Behind her, Dylan saw the teacher getting into her car and driving off. He just grinned.

'Well, I've always been up to something, haven't I?' he said.

The moment Dylan stepped inside the front door, Megs leapt six times her own height into his arms. He buried his face in her fur, mumbled something, rushed into the bedroom and slammed the door. As she tried to cover his whole face with licks, he breathed huge, shuddering breaths. He was safe, and Megs was safe, and nothing else could, or ever would, possibly matter.

Dylan sat in assembly with his shoulders hunched. The deafening sound of hundreds of people clapping and catcalling filled the room. He was too hot and the walls were creeping nearer, bunching everyone up, squashing all the smells of washing powder and shampoo and people into a dense fug.

It was horrible and boring being back at school, but the funny thing was, it didn't make him feel completely dead any more. Knowing that Lucia would love to be sitting right here made it impossible to hate it as much as he used to. He closed his eyes and pretended he was back on the Amazon, in those amazing few minutes when it was all his, and he was alone, with the rainforest behind him and the river moving silently along before him, with all of life and death contained in it. Now that he had the Amazon inside him, nothing mattered so much. Dylan had lost his bit of the river but he had found the Amazon and he would work out how to go back. And there was the Nile and the Mississippi and the Yangtse to see and somehow he would fix it so he could spend his whole life looking at rivers.

The Head stood on the stage with a huge grin on her face. She had just announced the winner of the Geography competition and was clapping the sixth former whose name she had called out. As soon as Dylan had copied and pasted all his texts into a report for Mr Shadid he had realised that Floyd was right. What he had written could double up as the Geography project. So he had emailed it to Mrs Hughes too. It would get him into plenty of trouble once the teachers showed his project to his parents, but at least he had done it. What would his parents do when they heard where he had really gone during half-term? What sort of punishment would you give a kid for going to the other end of the world? He would probably be grounded until he was thirty.

A sharp poke in the ribs made him look up. Matt was grinning like mad and nudging him. 'Looks like you've come second, Dyl.'

'Congratulations to Dylan Davies who chose, with great originality, to write a fictional account of the scandal which came to light recently about the highly regarded company, BlueBird. We have all read in the news about the shocking experiments involving homeless children, but Dylan's story – written as if in texts, answering his younger brother's questions, as if he was there at the time...' here she peered over the lectern until she found Dylan and smiled indulgently, 'bring the reality to life in a way that newspaper articles cannot hope to. He has clearly done an astonishing amount of research and recreates for us here in Wales an idea of what it must be like to actually be in the Amazon rainforest. It is the work of a truly outstanding imagination. It also includes some marvellous vocabulary, such as squander, gelid and pernickety. I particularly liked the phrase 'scandalising travesty of the highest order'. The Geography second prize goes to Dylan Davies, in Year Seven. Well done, Dylan.'

THIRTY-ONE

After school, Dylan picked up Megs and took a piece of toast with strawberry jam to Mum's computer and logged on to his email account. He had three hundred and seventeen unopened emails, mostly from bike shops and online sweet shops. Only one email was interesting. He clicked on it.

Today we are informed about physics. Radio waves most magical concept I ever apprehend

Dylan emailed back.

Physics? Magic? If you say so. I won a prize today, using your weird words.

That was it. Just a line a day between him and Lucia, an untouchable thread of words which held them together.

It would be a tight squeeze on the tree now that Joe was coming. Dylan and Megs sat at the far end of the fallen trunk, nearest the field. She was asleep on his lap, exhausted by the excitement of trying to wash Dylan all over with her tongue. She had clearly got over her fear of the fallen tree, which made Dylan think perhaps he could have another go at flying one day.

This was one of Dylan's last afternoons right here, where the tree bridged the river and the rope swing dangled over the busy waters below. The clocks would go back at the weekend and as rain was forecast for the rest of the week, it might be the last afternoon ever. Soon, his dad would tell him the news that they had to move and when the clocks went forward again, next Spring, they would be living somewhere in town.

Through the bare branches, Matt could be seen ambling up, hands in pockets, fishing for something. After him came Tommo, running. He caught up with Matt, who handed him something small from his pocket.

'Hey, Dylan, want a Starburst?' Matt called as he came closer. 'They pinned your project up on the English Language notice board, by the way. It's supposed to be an example of how to write a story.'

'Is Joe really coming today?' Tommo asked.

'Floyd said he'd bring him along after school. They'll be here soon.'

'Does he like … talking?' Tommo asked.

'What sort of a question is that?'

Tommo shrugged. 'I just sort of mean…'

'I think he'll be friendly, Tommo,' Dylan said.

Rob and Aled turned up, their long legs striding along in synch, as if they were on a slow-motion march. Dylan wondered if he would ever sit right where he was and see them coming towards him again.

'Did you really go in a private plane and a limo?' Aled asked.

'He ate a *whole tin* of mushrooms,' Tommo added, proudly. 'Without any mash.'

'Piranhas didn't eat you then?' Rob asked.

'No. We ate the piranhas,' Dylan said, boldly. He shuddered, remembering being inside the sack and the pointy teeth that bit into the leaf. No point telling them it had been quite close at one point.

'You should be dead,' Matt said. 'That guy with the butterflies, he woulda killed you dead if it wasn't for that kid.' He shook his head.

Dylan couldn't see Floyd yet, but he was sure he would get here soon. He had to come. He had to have everyone here, on the fallen tree, all together for possibly the last time in his life. He nudged Matt.

'Didn't think I could do it, did you?'

'Do what?'

'Get there, get back, get us all here together.'

'I thought you were mad. I still think you're mad. You are mad. It was a stupid idea. Fact that it's worked is just pure fluke. You've used up all your luck for your whole life. If I were you I wouldn't risk so much as looking at a ladder ever again, let alone walking under one.' Matt shook his head and glanced at Dylan. 'And now you'll be the Geography teacher's and the English teacher's pet. How am I supposed to put up with that?'

'Hey!' Floyd's voice called out from among the trees. 'This is Joe. This is his first day out of bed. He's going to be starting school with you, Tommo, next week.'

Tommo shuffled closer to Dylan on the tree.

'There's room here,' Tommo said, his voice full of hope.

'Pass him over,' Dylan said, 'give him a hand, Aled, Matt, he can step between your legs.'

Joe looked up at Floyd, who nodded at him and handed him over. When Joe had been handed across everyone's legs, he sat down next to Tommo and stared at the water between his legs.

'I can whistle,' Tommo said. He pursed his lips together and a breathy, wobbly warble came out.

Joe looked at Tommo very seriously. 'I can click my fingers,' he said. He held his hands up and clicked his thumbs against his middle fingers to demonstrate.

Tommo nodded slowly. 'That's cool.' He held one hand up and tried.

'Like this,' Joe said, showing him which finger to use. Tommo gave it a go and made no noise.

'Faster,' Joe said. 'And harder.'

From across everyone's heads, Dylan caught Floyd's eye. They glanced at their younger brothers and grinned. And as Floyd grinned, Dylan understood exactly what it was that ran in Floyd's veins. It was obvious. Floyd's veins ran clear with water. Simple, clean ordinary water. Not complicated, dangerous or exciting. But something you needed every single day. How had Dylan not guessed that? They were real friends now, the sort that could nod at each other across a crowded school corridor and feel as if they had had a whole conversation.

Since the first day of secondary school, Dylan had wanted them all to be together by the river, sitting on the fallen tree, and now they were. And the fact that it wasn't going to last, or maybe ever happen again, made him feel as if he was in a photograph, one he would look at over and over again. Every detail – each branch and twig and mossy bit of bark and splash of water, and everyone's face – was sharp and bright and the colours were practically singing.

'It's a Lamborghini,' Tommo was saying, showing Joe a small yellow car. 'I've got a red one, too.'

Joe leaned over to one side and fished around in his trouser pocket for something.

'Maserati,' he said, pulling out the blue car. 'Maseratis have beaten Lamborghinis in the Grand Prix every year for ten years.'

The two boys stared at each other for a few moments. Tommo gulped and blinked. Then he nudged Joe and grinned.

'No, they haven't,' he said. 'You're making that up!' And Joe laughed and shoved Tommo back a bit until they were both laughing and tussling and pretending to push each other off.

'Dylan, I'm glad to catch you on your own. Come here a minute, will you? I want to talk to you.' His dad stood on the riverbank.

'Come and sit here, Dad.' Dylan said. He stroked Megs and felt her sigh under his touch. He wanted one memory of him and his dad sitting on the fallen tree too before it was all over. The last few minutes of his last evening were running out. Dylan knew that, and it still made him sad, but it wasn't the cold dark pain it had been a few weeks ago.

'I've been outside all day, Dylan. All I want to do is sit in front of the telly.' But his dad took a step closer.

'Please, Dad. You'll like it.'

Dylan's dad sighed and took easy strides onto the tree. He stood on it, looking behind him, up river, then to the front, down river.

'Sit down, Dad.' Dylan felt a new power. Dylan's body

was pretty much the same size as it had been at the beginning of term, but inside he felt as grown up as his dad.

His dad crouched, then sat on the trunk, letting his legs dangle over the river. Dylan said nothing for a while. If he could just put it off for a few more moments.

'There's the robin that always sits on that branch. And you see that overhanging bit of grass there? Down by the water? A creature lives in there. A vole or something. It slithers in and out and you can just see it sometimes.'

'This is a good place,' his dad said, but you could tell that the word 'good' didn't cover what he really felt. Dylan sensed the oil in his dad's veins flowing more freely.

'Mesmerising looking at the water, isn't it? I can see how you like playing here.'

'It's not playing, Dad,' Dylan said. 'It's...' What was it? How could he describe it? 'It's ... being real.'

'Sitting here on your own?'

'With Megs and everyone. I'm hardly ever here on my own.'

'Yes, you're a pack animal, aren't you? There's something about this water rushing by. You can't see the road from here. Or the farm. It could be the Middle Ages and you wouldn't be able to tell.'

Dylan said nothing. The magic was working. Dad had forgotten about the telly. He wasn't even tired any more. A tawny owl hooted in the distance. But Dylan knew he couldn't put it off forever. It was best to get it over and done with. He took a deep breath and spoke in a completely normal voice.

'What was it you wanted to talk to me about?' he asked. This was the moment. He felt sorry for Dad, having to tell him this news. But Dylan would be so cool about it that Dad would think he didn't mind at all. He had all his words ready.

'Oh that,' his dad said, pushing his rough hair back over his forehead. 'Yes. I'll need your help next summer, Dylan. I'll get you doing some work on the farm and pay you.'

'On the farm?' Dylan looked sharply at his dad. 'On what farm?'

His dad looked at him oddly. 'Where do think, you great mush? Here, on our farm of course. Actually, things were looking iffy for a while, but Owen came through with some good news this morning. We're going to buy the farm, lad. There were some new buyers, but they've decided to sell to us. Don't know what changed their minds, but I'm not asking questions. They said something about seeing the smaller picture, and how each tree is a home to hundreds of creatures. And something completely garbled about a robin.'

Dylan didn't move. You couldn't tell anything from the outside. From the outside he looked like an eleven-year-old, sitting unusually still on a fallen tree. But inside him the volcano erupted in frothing lava, crushing his breath, making his ears fizz, effervescing, exploding, setting off fireworks in his brain. He sat in silence, blinking, until his throat felt normal enough to speak.

'Cool,' he said, nodding. 'I'd be up for that.' The two branches of a nearby tree stretched their arms out towards him, beckoning him, begging for a treehouse, and he grinned.

There was only one small problem left.

'Dad,' he said. 'You know that … er, story I wrote for the Geography prize?'

'Yes?'

'There's something I want to tell you.'

ACKNOWLEDGEMENTS

So many people helped in the writing of this story and I'm hugely grateful for all their wonderful ideas.

Thank you to Sarah Levison of Golden Egg who mentored me through the story – and thought up the title – and to the whole Golden Egg community, which has been such a delight. Imogen Cooper has created a world of her own. Thank you also to Penny, Rebecca and Megan at Firefly Press for taking me on and offering guidance, support and friendship. I'm so proud to be a Firefly.

I met some boys on the plane to Lisbon – Casper Kingsley, Rafael Leon Villapalos and Gianlucia Cristofoli-Quinn – who kindly gave me their perspective on the Amazon and on reading in general. Thanks to Jono and Caroline at Nomadic Thoughts who arranged a perfectly balanced research trip, and to Philippa Vernon-Powell and Evelyn FitzHerbert for their encouragement. Roberto Mercês, my excellent guide around the city of Salvador and around the communities, gently relieved me of my ignorance and told me about Carolina Maria de Jesus' book, *Child of the Dark*, which made me more confident about my idea for Lucia's character. Profesora Marijane of Escola Aberta in the Salvador community very kindly showed me around her beautiful school. I'm grateful to the people of the Mamiraua Sustainable Development Reserve for sharing their part of the Amazonian rainforest and river and to Gabriel Gomes for his guidance. Sonia and Fernanda Carvalho's friendship and help at the reserve made the whole trip a joy.

Thank you to James Nicol and Malachy Doyle for timely advice. My wonderful writing group – Sandra MacDonald, Janine Scoggins, Mellany Ambrose, Sulin Dow, Eileen Aird – were invaluable in offering ideas and comments and for steering me away from dull patches. I've had brilliant insights from Elizabeth Bazalgette, Kirsty Hollings and Katherine Louise Price and I could not have described the digger accurately without the help and demo from our young neighbour, Mabôn Sion. Thank you, Mum, for your constant encouragement and thank you to Hamish, Dougal, Matilda and especially Mathew for absolutely everything.

If you want to find out more, take a look at *Child of the Dark* by Carolina Maria de Jesus and at wwwprojetoaxe.org/brasil